Edmund P. Dole

The Stand-By

A novel

Edmund P. Dole

The Stand-By
A novel

ISBN/EAN: 9783337030230

Printed in Europe, USA, Canada, Australia, Japan

Cover: Foto ©Andreas Hilbeck / pixelio.de

More available books at **www.hansebooks.com**

THE STAND-BY

BY

EDMUND P. DOLE

Author of "Talks about Law"

NEW YORK
THE CENTURY CO.
1897

CONTENTS

PART ONE—ANTE-BELLUM

PART TWO—THE FIRST CAMPAIGN

PART THREE—THE LEAGUE

THE STAND-BY

PART ONE

ANTE-BELLUM

THE STAND-BY

I

CRIMSON AND BLUE

THERE had been excuses without end. There always are when defeats seem disgraceful. They said that their new shell had been too light; that the water had been rough; that they had had the course across the eel-grass. The Yale crew had lost its race by many lengths, and had become an object of ridicule in the public press.

Harvard was laden with boating honors. The crew that had won a large share of them, and had left Yale almost out of sight, was to row with her again.

But Yale was hopeful, if not confident. Her undergraduates and thousands of her alumni knew that if she was beaten it would be honorable defeat. The sporting fraternity and the general public believed that Harvard would win, but they expected that Yale would fight hard enough to make it a great race, and even Harvard men admitted that it might be close.

"You see, Senator Clifford," said Tom Andrews,—
and he voiced the general opinion,—"you see, we
would n't have had a ghost of a show if it had n't been
for the 'Stand-by.' Harvard has a veteran crew, but
we 've got the captain. He 's all brains and sand.
He won't make any errors, and he will keep every man
in his shell up to his work for every ounce of muscle
there is in him from start to finish."

The day was perfect. The broad expanse of water,
unruffled by a breeze, glistened in the sunlight like
burnished silver. All things favored a fair trial of
strength and skill.

From their quarters, a mile or more above, the rival
crews swept down the river, not at speed, but with
a good, swinging stroke that started the sweat and
limbered their muscles.

In addition to the cockswains they numbered sixteen
men, picked from many hundred. For months they
had worked to gain strength and endurance. For
months they had rowed, at first in the gymnasium
tanks, then, when spring came, on the harbor and the
river. For weeks they had retired at ten, and had
eaten at the training-table. For the time being, like
Samson and Hercules, they were men set apart from
their fellows, selected to uphold in a brief but agonizing contest the honor of two great universities.

They were greeted with deafening cheers from the
"movable grand stand," the long train of platform-
cars that lined the west bank of the river.

"'Rah, 'rah, 'rah! 'Rah, 'rah, 'rah! 'Rah, 'rah, 'rah!
'Arvard!" yelled hundreds of Cambridge under-gradu-
ates, in perfect time.

"Harvard, Harvard, Harvard!" shouted their thousands of friends.

Distinct as the voice of one man, loud as a peal of thunder, came the answering cry: "Breke-kek-ex ko-ax ko-ax! Breke-kek-ex ko-ax ko-ax! O op, O op, parabalou! Yale!"

"'Rah, 'rah, 'rah! 'Rah, 'rah, 'rah! 'Rah, 'rah, 'rah! Yale!" shouted thousands who wore the blue.

"Hic, hæc, hoc! Hug-us, hug-us, hug-us! Yum, yum! Smack, smack! Vassar-r-r!" piped a mischievous ventriloquist, as the roar died away.

The boats took their places.

It was the moment of sickening dread that comes before battle, but every man in the crews sat rigid and quiet, ready to fight for the last inch, even when overwrought muscles were thrilling with agony and an instant's respite was relief from supreme torture.

"Are you ready?" There was a quiet response from each boat, and then the crack of a pistol.

At the pistol's flash eight sinewy bodies bent to their work for the glory of the crimson, and eight for the glory of the blue. Harvard started with a magnificent spurt and instantly took the lead. Yale followed with thirty-two long, strong, uniform strokes to the minute. For a mile the distance between the boats did not perceptibly change.

The platform-cars, with their thousands of spectators, kept opposite the rowers, and ever and again cheers burst forth like salvos of artillery: "'Rah, 'rah, 'rah! 'Rah, 'rah, 'rah! 'Rah, 'rah, 'rah! 'Arvard!" "Breke-kek-ex ko-ax ko-ax! Breke-kek-ex ko-ax ko-ax! O op, O op, parabalou! Yale!" "Harvard, Harvard, Harvard!" "Yale, Yale, Yale!" The excitement became intense.

Harvard maintained her lead till the second half of the second mile, when she made a spurt, putting her more than a length ahead.

The spurt was good generalship. It seemed to presage easy victory. It disheartened Yale's friends. It set Harvard's wild with enthusiasm. The cheers for Harvard were deafening. The cries for Yale were like a wail of despair. It was a terrible ordeal for a new crew rowing against veterans flushed with victory, an ordeal that nothing but indomitable will, iron discipline, and perfect confidence in a leader could sustain. A momentary discouragement, the least relaxation of effort on the part of a single man, and Yale's chance was hopelessly lost.

It was good generalship when Napoleon hurled his Old Guard to foam itself away against the British squares at Waterloo, for on a hundred battle-fields it had carried all before it; but Englishmen and Scotchmen were there to stay—as conquerors or as corpses.

At the end of the third mile Yale had raised her stroke a trifle and was scarcely a length behind. Both sides cheered frantically.

In the first quarter of the fourth and last mile Yale spurted and began to creep up; but Harvard again quickened, and the gain was lost.

In the last half Harvard began to show the exhausting effect of her tremendous spurts, and her stroke became ragged.

"Our boys have won the race all right," said Harvard men, "but if there 's sand enough left in those fellows to make a handsome spurt, we won't have much to spare."

"We 've still got a show," replied Yale men, "and the Stand-by 'll fight her for all there is in it."

"Now," said the Yale captain to his crew, "a spurt to the finish!"

In that low, quiet tone was the fierce joy of conflict and the inspiration of victory. The response came from bare, brown, sinewy arms. Breath was too precious for words. There was no sound save the quick, regular dipping of the spoons, and the rushing of the water, and the wild cheers from the west shore. Under those long, powerful strokes the shell seemed to rise like a flying-fish and fairly leap through the water.

Harvard had made three great spurts, the last in the last two minutes. It was not in flesh and blood to make another so soon. Yale was gaining steadily; then she touched—barely touched—a mass of floating seaweed. It delayed her only an instant, but that instant brought the loss, as it seemed, of her only chance.

The rival crew so regarded it, and rowed with more confidence. The spectators so understood it, and "'Rah, 'rah, 'rah! 'Rah, 'rah, 'rah! 'Rah, 'rah, 'rah! 'Arvard!" burst forth like a peal of thunder.

An expression of ghastly despair flitted over the faces of the Yale crew. "Now!" exclaimed their captain, and his voice, though low, stirred them like a trumpet. The expression of despair vanished. His spirit had recovered full possession of them—the spirit that in the supreme moment counts life nothing, victory everything. There was no flurry. The thirty-six strokes to the minute had the regularity, sweep, and power of the thirty-two.

Seconds passed. The cheering was continuous now, the excitement was so intense. The boats were prow and prow, and the finish was only half a dozen rods away.

As the Yale cockswain glanced at his captain he saw that his face looked drawn; but the eyes themselves were bright, the teeth were set, the stroke did not falter, and the iron muscles still bent the strong oar like a reed.

A moment later the boats swept past the line, Yale three feet ahead, and her captain fell back into the arms of the man behind him.

The honor of a great university was redeemed. It was worth living for. It was worth dying for.

Smooth-checked freshmen, dignified seniors, and gray-haired alumni, wild with excitement, rushed down to the water to watch the crew as it boarded the college launch. Anxiously, tenderly, proudly, the captain was taken aboard.

From the harbor the guns of the yachts thundered their salutes, but louder and longer and wilder than the thunders of the cannon rose the cry from twenty thousand throats: "'Rah, 'rah, 'rah! 'Rah, 'rah, 'rah! 'Rah, 'rah, 'rah! Yale!"

II

MISS DENMAN

"YOU see," said Tom Andrews, "chum was n't a boating man at first. We made him try for the crew because we all knew there was n't any one else who could bring out as he could the full strength of every oar just when it was needed most. It 's a way he has of managing men."

"Which means winning the battle of life," remarked Senator Clifford.

"There 's no knowing what he 'll be one of these days," continued Tom. "He 's the most popular man in the class, and a Bones man."

"What 's a Bones man?" asked Miss Clifford, a rather plain young lady with a pleasant face.

"That 's what I 'd like to know," said Tom. "It 's a senior society, the most select and mysterious of the college societies. He is n't enough of a dig to be valedictorian, but he 'll win the De Forest, and that 's a great deal better."

"What is the De Forest?" inquired Mrs. Clifford.

"It 's the best Townsend."

9

"And what is a Townsend?"

"The six best writers and speakers in the senior class get the Townsend prizes, and the best of the six gets the De Forest. It's the highest literary honor a Yale man can win. Craigin is one of the best writers in our class, and the best speaker."

"He certainly has a warm advocate in you, Tom," said Mrs. Clifford.

"Why should n't he have? He'd stand by me to the death. He's the Stand-by. That's what we all call him, and we fellows size each other up pretty well, Mrs. Clifford. He would n't go back on a friend if a pack of wolves were at his throat. He's the whitest man I know, and as brainy and brave as Uncle John Denman."

"Thank you!" interrupted the beautiful girl.

"That's all right, Isabel! We know you think there never was any one else in the world like your father; but I tell you, Craigin's more like him in some ways than you'd believe, with all your gift for reading people."

"Why, Tom, I was n't sarcastic. I was glad you spoke that way about papa and your friend."

"You see, Senator Clifford," continued Tom, returning to his eulogy, "we fellows all feel that Craigin is different from the rest of us—lives on a higher plane, as Prex would say. He's a little stiff and cranky in some of his notions—at least you'd think so, and we think so; but we don't like him any the less for it, for there is n't a bit of cant about him, and we all know if he thought a thing was right he'd stand by it, life or death, and never flinch a hair."

"I'd like—" began the old statesman.

He did n't finish the sentence, for at that moment several hundred college men, in the halls and corridors of the hotel and in the streets close by, struck up their songs :

"Oh! the bulldog on the bank,
   And the bullfrog in the pool;
Oh! the bulldog on the bank,
   And the bullfrog in the pool;
Oh! the bulldog on the bank,
   And the bullfrog in the pool;
The bulldog called the bullfrog
   A great big water fool.

       " Singing,
Shool, shool, shool I rool,
Shool I shag-a-rack, shool-a-barb-a-cool,
   The first time I saw her,
Shool I bally eel,
Dis cum bibble lola boo, slow reel.

"Saw my leg off,
   Saw my leg off,
      Saw my leg off
         Short!

"A boy he had an auger
   That bored two holes at once;
A boy he had an auger
   That bored two holes at once;
And we buried him in the lowlands, lowlands,
         lowlands,
   And we buried him in the lowlands, low!

"Old Noah he did build an ark,
   Luddy, fuddy, oh! poor luddy, heigh-ho!
To sail about in Central Park.
   Luddy, fuddy, oh! poor luddy, fuddy!
   Oh! luddy, fuddy, poor luddy, heigh-ho!"

After serenading the hotel for fifteen or twenty minutes they started out through the town. Hundreds of students marched up and down the streets, singing their songs and yelling, "Breke-kek-ex ko-ax ko-ax! Breke-kek-ex ko-ax ko-ax! O op, O op, parabalou! Craigin!" Hundreds of men who were not up in "The Frogs" of Aristophanes, from graduates of forty years' standing to the relatives and friends of mere freshmen, joined the procession, shouting at the top of their voices, "'Rah, 'rah, 'rah! 'Rah, 'rah, 'rah! 'Rah, 'rah, 'rah! Yale!"

"Tom," said the senator, "I wish we might meet your friend."

"I 'd set my heart on it," replied Tom. "I spoke to the doctor about it awhile ago, and he said he thought it would be all right in an hour or so. I 'll go and see now."

In about fifteen minutes a shout came from the hotel office, "Here 's Craigin." The few bystanders took it up. The news passed from lip to lip as beacon-lights flash from hill to hill, and from the marching hosts down the street and from every part of the little city, filled to overflowing with friends of old Yale, came the exultant cry, "Craigin 's all right! 'Rah for Craigin! 'Rah for the Stand-by!" The procession headed down street turned about. In a few minutes the hotel was packed and surrounded with thousands of men, shouting, "What 's the matter with Craigin? He 's all right!" Five, ten, fifteen minutes passed, and the hubbub showed no signs of abating. Every now and then the senator and his party heard single voices shouting, "How are you, Craigin?" "Bully for you, Craigin!" "God bless you, Craigin!" and then single voices were drowned in a mighty roar.

At last Tom returned with the hero of the day. "Senator and Mrs. Clifford," he said, "allow me to present my friend Mr. Craigin; Miss Clifford, Mr. Craigin; my cousin Miss Denman, Mr. Craigin."

Craigin had exchanged his rowing costume—as nearly Adam's as decency permitted—for a fashionably cut and perfectly fitting summer suit of rough navy blue. His ordinary weight of about two hundred pounds had been reduced by training to one hundred and seventy-five, and by the terrible contest through which he had just passed to one hundred and sixty-seven. He was five feet ten in height, straight as an arrow, and of remarkable figure. His feet were rather small than otherwise, his legs compact and shapely, but not large. From the hips down there was nothing striking in the outlines of his person. From the hips up he thickened like a double wedge. His shoulders were immensely broad in proportion to his hips, and his chest was correspondingly full and deep. Another peculiarity was the extraordinary length of his arms. As the senator grasped the young man's hand he noticed that, though small, it was hard, almost like iron, and that the large wrist was like the pastern of a thoroughbred trotter. The old man had a keen eye for points in sporting matters as well as in things legal and political. "H'm!" he said to himself, "the youngster could strike a knock-down blow with John L. Sullivan."

If the "youngster" resembled the world's late champion in length and strength of arms and in massiveness

of chest and shoulders, there was no hint of the prize-
fighter in the noble face and head that crowned them.
It was a strong face, distinguished-looking rather than
handsome, with a determined chin, a beautiful and
sensitive mouth, a broad upper lip covered with a
brown mustache, a fine nose, and clear blue eyes. He
was evidently a blond, but training in the hot sun had
made his skin for the time being a mass of tan and
freckles.

For a moment they looked into each other's eyes—
the hero of that great race, whose friend had declared
him brainy and brave as John Denman, and John
Denman's daughter, whose beauty would have distinguished her among thousands. But more striking
than her beauty were Miss Denman's inimitable grace
of motion, and the strong, proud character manifest in
her radiant features and large dark eyes.

"We came over from Newport to see the race, and
have n't been disappointed," said the senator. "We
did n't have anything like this in my college days.
They say it 's the best on record. I congratulate you,
Mr. Craigin."

"I 'm glad Yale can accept congratulations," replied
Craigin. "But honors are about even, Senator Clifford
—only three feet difference in four miles." -

The terribly dry, choking sensation, and the feeling
of having been rasped internally from lungs to throat,
were gradually passing away; but the athlete's voice,
naturally clear as a silver bell, still trembled and was
broken and husky. There was a pallor under his brown
skin, and under his eyes were large black circles. How
could it be otherwise? He had put his life into that race.

Senator Clifford noticed it, and the modesty of the young man's bearing and answer. It was the bearing of one accustomed to good society and perfectly self-possessed, yet evidently flattered by an introduction to the famous statesman.

"Ah!" said the senator, "that won't do! I gave you a non-negotiable congratulation, as we lawyers would put it, one you can't indorse over to Yale and Harvard. The others did well, but I 'm enough of a sporting man, Mr. Craigin, to know that you won that race only by putting your own brains and your own life against victory. You see, they all understand it," he remarked, as his voice was drowned by the deep, harsh, guttural cry, in perfect time, from hundreds of students in the street below: "Breke-kek-ex ko-ax ko-ax! Breke-kek-ex ko-ax ko-ax! O op, O op, para-balou! Craigin!"

The conversation became general, and, sitting opposite Miss Denman, Craigin forgot all about his triumph and that he was under the doctor's care.

While the carriage was waiting to take the Cliffords and Miss Denman to their train the senator took Craigin aside for a little private conversation.

"My boy," he said, "I 'm very glad I 've met you. If you 'll permit it, I want to say that I 've taken to you greatly. I like you; I believe in you. I hope the time will come when I can serve you."

"I 'm very glad, proud, to have you feel that way toward me."

"Tom says you 're going into journalism."

"Yes, I 've intended to for a long time."

"If you are satisfied that that 's your vocation, I

don't know as I would want to influence you against it if I could; but I'm an old man, and have seen a great deal of the world, and I know you'll take it as kindly as I mean it if I suggest something for you to think over."

"I certainly will. I shall be very thankful."

"You're not a man for a subordinate position, to be a mere editorial writer; and the managing editor of a great paper is the slave of the counting-house, of private interests and political expediency. He can't have a nice conscience and be a success."

"Do you think so?"

"I know so. He can't be honest any more than a politician can be, nor half as much."

"But, Senator Clifford, you're a politician, and everybody, even your enemies, says you're honest."

"Because I'm honest according to the world's standard. I never had a dollar that was n't fairly mine, never was false to a client, never went back on the Republican party, and I think I never lost a good chance to give the Democrats hot shot—that's my religion; and, as to the rest, I take the world pretty much as I find it. I've got a low standard, don't profess anything else, and live up to it. You've got a high standard, and I believe you live up to it. One reason I take to you so much is because I've found the genuine article of your grade scarce as hen's teeth; and another is because I love a fighter—all the world loves a fighter."

"Do you think it's easier to get on with a nice conscience in law than it is as a managing editor?"

"A hundred times. It may handicap a young lawyer at first, but there's a class of clients in business centers who are willing to pay large fees for absolute honesty with brains and learning, and the profession demands such men for the bench."

"Senator Clifford," said Miss Denman, returning and laying her gloved hand on his shoulder, "the train goes in seven minutes. If we don't start now we shall all be left."

"Gad! is n't she a bird?" exclaimed one of Craigin's classmates, thirty seconds later, as Craigin handed her into the carriage.

"A bird!" retorted another. "I say a pair of birds! And a finer pair never was mated."

That night Craigin left the banquet early by doctor's orders, and went to bed and slept, and in his dreams there came to him, not the mighty voice of thousands of men shouting his praises, but a few and simple words of a girl of seventeen.

III

ON THE "MYRA-GLADYS"

THE Earl and Countess of Throckmorton and their two sons, Viscount Stadwick and the Hon. Mr. Langdon, on their yachting trip along the coast, stopped over a few days at Newport. Years before the earl, as British ambassador, and Senator Clifford, as American minister, had represented their respective governments at one of the great European capitals. The acquaintance there formed had ripened into an intimate friendship, and so it happened that when they met at Newport, just after the great regatta, the senatorial party changed their plans and went yachting with the earl's up the coast of Labrador.

The senator had spent his boyhood on a rocky New England farm. He had worked his way through college by swinging his scythe in summer and teaching district schools in winter. Unaided he had struggled to front rank in his profession and to leadership in American politics. His distinction was personal. No son could inherit it. Even his modest fortune was almost sure to be scattered or lost in the second or third generation. He was a representative product of democratic institutions, as his friend was of a great and

18

proud aristocracy—the one of the man that dies, the other of the family that goes on from age to age.

For the gigantic, fat, red-faced, red-whiskered, red-headed, jolly old Englishman, who wore a slouch-hat and pea-jacket and smoked a corn-cob pipe on board his yacht, and played ring-toss as merrily as a boy and whist as seriously as if the fate of empires hung on it, was one of the shrewdest statesmen, one of the richest and most blue-blooded noblemen, in Europe, with a pedigree crossing royal lines and stretching back into the dark ages.   The Cliffords and Isabel Denman well knew how much of a personage he was, and that the big, handsome young viscount, who was so attentive to them all, especially to Isabel, as surely as he lived would one day be one of the greatest of English peers.

The days passed swiftly as they skirted the coast of Labrador.   A rugged coast, indented with bays and inlets and fine, deep harbors.   "Dark and yellow headlands towering over the waters, some grim and naked, others clear in the pale green of mosses and dwarf shrubbery.   Rocky precipices, fantastic and picturesque in form, with stony vales winding alway among the blue hills of the interior."   Islands, islands everywhere!   Majestic icebergs, slowly drifting southward, gleaming under the sunlight and under the moonlight in all the colors of the rainbow, like huge prisms!

Stopping now and then at points of interest,—Battle Harbor, Ivuktoka, Point Rigoulette, Cape Webuck, Cape Chudleigh,—the party spent a month cruising to the northernmost confines of the great peninsula and back again.   A month is a long time when young men and maidens are together on a pleasure-yacht.   They played games; they sang songs; they danced, Mrs. Clifford playing the piano and the old earl the fiddle. When the fog settled down and there was nothing to see, they improvised a little farce, and read the same books. Most delightful of all were the moonlight evenings, when they sat on deck wrapped in furs, and talked and sang and gazed on the grand, stern outlines of the desolate land and the ever-changing sea and the glory of the northern heavens.

Long before the voyage was ended Isabel knew, though no word had been spoken, that the heir to that great earldom loved her with his whole heart, and realized that she was beginning to like him better than any other young man she had ever met.

"Getting serious, is n't it?" observed the earl, one night as they were skirting the Maine coast on their return.

"I'm glad of it, John," replied the countess; "she'll be a woman among thousands—only—"

"Only what?"

"Only I wish she was n't a brewer's daughter!"

"So do I!" exclaimed the earl. "It may be class prejudice, but in spite of all Clifford says about the man, I can't help it."

Isabel read their hearts like an open book—the joy with which they would welcome her as a daughter, the distaste, which they supposed so carefully concealed, for her father's plebeian occupation. It stung her to the quick.

"He's a brewer," she said to herself, "but he's John Denman. I've never seen a man to stand beside him —unless—unless it's the Stand-by."

IV

T was senior vacation. Craigin was a De Forest, and in three weeks would be a B. A. and enter the great race of life. Examinations had closed that day, and he and Andrews were spending one of their last evenings together in the old room in South College.

"Tom," he said, "you're always talking about Apsleigh; what sort of a place is it to live in?"

"A daisy. Why?"

"That's the why," replied Craigin, tossing his roommate a letter.

Tom read as follows:

MR. WILLIAM H. CRAIGIN.

DEAR SIR: Our present editor is about to leave, and one of your professors, an old friend and classmate of mine, says we shall be extremely fortunate if we can get you to take his place. There is one other Republican daily, the "Times," in our little city. It is the oldest and one of the ablest papers in the State. The "Tocsin" is a new paper, intended to voice more positive convictions of right and wrong than the "Times" appears to have, to lead rather than follow, and represent principles rather than spoils. Of course we have a good deal to contend with.

2*   21

We can't pay you more than a hundred and fifty dollars a month until we get on a better financial basis. We could not think of offering you even that if it were not for the exceptionally good things said of you. Will you come and see us?

Very sincerely yours,
Henry Harnett,
President of Tocsin Publishing Co.

"That 's just your kind of paper," said Andrews, as he finished reading the letter.

"Then you 'd say go, would n't you?"

Tom smoked reflectively for many minutes before replying: "If you want my advice, Billy, don't go; don't have anything to do with it."

"Why not?"

"Because, as sure as you do, sooner or later you 'll lock horns with Uncle John."

"Well?"

"You won't say whatever the almighty dollar tells you; you 'll say what you honestly think."

"Of course, if I go."

"And you can't edit that kind of a paper in that State without getting mixed up with the liquor question."

"Well?"

"Well, Uncle John, as you know, has a big brewery, a big wholesale and retail liquor house, the two leading hotels in Apsleigh, and controls the liquor business in all that part of the State. He 's worth several millions; but it is n't money gives him his grip so much as the kind of man he is. He 's one of the bravest, most generous, tenderest-hearted old fellows on earth. It is n't the money he gives so much as the way he gives it, the good will that goes with it, the kind, beautiful, Christ-like things he's doing all the time— see?"

"Yes."

"And he stands for just what cranks like you don't believe in, making the liquor business decent instead of trying to destroy it. They've had the stiffest kind of a prohibitory law up there for twenty years—on paper —and all the law that amounts to anything is Uncle John. If a man stands in with him and keeps a decent place he knows he's all right, and he knows he'll have to shut up pretty d—d quick if he sells to children and drunken men and has rows and knock-downs and drag-outs. For years and years the city governments that have had these things in charge have been Uncle John's shadow."

"Suppose we speak of him as his Royal Highness, John, King of Apsleigh," suggested Craigin. "'T is n't democratic, but it seems to hit the case as you put it."

"That's what they call him, 'King of Apsleigh,' and I tell you, mighty few kings sit their thrones as he does his. People love him. Then, since the great railroad fight, they don't believe anybody can down him. The railroad folks thought they had him where they could squeeze him dry, and it ended with the railroad in his breeches pocket. Those 'Tocsin' people know how good-natured he is, that he'll stand what most men with his power would n't and give way in little things, and of course they'll want to press what they call reforms as far as he'll let 'em; but if it should come to a fight, a peasant would as soon think of standing up against the Czar of all the Russias. That's where they are n't like you. It 'll come to a fight if you go there, and he 'll break you as he broke the railroad—that 's why I say, don't go."

"Tom," inquired Craigin, pacing the floor, and writing an imaginary letter on his left palm with the forefinger of his right hand, "Tom, how does this sound?

'Hon. Henry Harnett.

'Dear Sir: Your favor is just received. The salary is more than I hoped for at first, and the position highly satisfactory; in fact, I expected to begin as a reporter. It has been my ambition to be connected with a paper that has positive convictions of right and wrong and the courage to stand by them, that leads rather than follows, and represents principles rather than spoils. I would, therefore, gladly accept your offer were I not informed that such a paper might offend the richest and most influential man in your city. Under the circumstances, I think it will be safer and in every way better for me to find a community where I can edit a paper of high moral tone and positive convictions without offending anybody.'

Tom, suppose I should put that in black and white and send it to Mr. Harnett? What would he think of me? What would the professor who has written to him think of me?"

"They 'd despise you, of course."

"Despise me! The lowest party hack would despise me as a coward and a hypocrite. Yet it 's only putting your suggestion into plain English. Tom, the first principle of honesty is honesty with one's self. I won't act on motives that I can't put in black and white and publish to the world without shame."

"That 's awfully pretty in theory," observed Tom.

"A theory does n't amount to Hannah Cook," replied Craigin, "if it is n't true, if it won't stand the test of living up to."

"It 's pretty to look at and talk about," continued Tom, "but it does n't wash in real life. If you idealists could agree, and were as brave and self-sacrificing as you talk, there 's nothing you could n't do; but you 're the only one of 'em I ever saw, if you thought it a duty to stand on a railroad track, would stay there and let a train run over you. I 'll admit it 's sublime, though to common people like me it looks a good deal like suicide."

"Well?"

"Well, Uncle John 's made of the same kind of stuff you are, only he has n't your principles and would n't be handicapped with conscientious scruples. I 've no doubt some of the 'Tocsin' people have principles as radical as yours, and if they feel very strong and brave maybe they 'll help you stir up the old lion; but when it comes to the crunching of bones they won't be there."

"Crunching of bones! Tom, these men, for the public good and with hardly a chance of profit, have put their money into what 's as risky as a gold-mine, and they offer to pay me more than they can afford because they think I 'll stand by 'em. I think I see myself, without a dollar of my own at stake, telling 'em between the lines they 'll run away when it comes to a crunching of bones!"

For the first time in all their long comradeship Andrews threw his arms around Craigin's neck and kissed his forehead. "Chum," he cried pathetically, "you know how proud I am of you. We all are, here.

We all know that you will be a famous man, a great man, a useful man, if you don't let your quixotic notions of duty run away with your common sense. We 've been like brothers for seven years, chum, and I love you better than any one else in the world except my mother, and next to you I love Uncle John. As sure as you go, chum, I know there 'll misery come of it. Don't go!"

"I can't promise you to-night, old man," said Craigin, greatly touched; "I must sleep on it."

"I know just how it 'll be," replied Andrews, sadly; "you 'll sleep on it all right enough, and think it all over, and the more chance there is of struggle and sacrifice for an ideal, the more you 'll persuade yourself it 's your duty. I know it is n't a bit of use, but I can't help saying, don't go!"

Two days later Craigin packed his bag and started for Apsleigh.

V

CRAIGIN accepted the position at a salary of two thousand dollars, half in treasury stock at sixty cents on the dollar. He found that Tom had not exaggerated Denman's power, and that the desire to maintain a paper with positive convictions was seasoned with a reasonable degree of worldly caution. Some of the stockholders also seemed to be influenced quite as much by hostility to the "Times" and other personal motives as by a wish to promote the public good.

In talking over the purpose and policy of the paper, the liquor question came up.

"It was established," said Mr. Harnett, "to represent the best wing of the Republican party. It is n't a temperance organ in the sense that the 'Congregationalist,' for example, is a sectarian organ, though of course it 's on that side."

"I 'd much rather it would be as it is," replied Craigin. "I could n't edit a paper as a lawyer pleads a cause, regardless of his own convictions. I believe in prohibition where public sentiment will sustain it.

I can't say yet that I believe in it as a hard and fast rule.
I have n't had a chance to think it out for myself."

Craigin was charmed with Apsleigh. As Andrews
had said, it was a daisy. On the afternoon of the
second day he saw a crowd collecting on one of the
principal streets, and joined it.

"He's a beauty, hain't he?" exclaimed an old farmer.

"Harnsomest colt in the State," replied a flashy man,
with the positive tone of self-made authority.

"Too much of the old man in him for a hoss," said
another.

"'F he sets up his Ebenezer ag'in' John Denman
there'll be music, let me tell ye," prophesied a fourth.

Craigin gradually worked his way through the crowd
to the front. The animal referred to was a stallion of
price and pedigree, large, powerful, spirited, matchless
in form, black as midnight, beautiful as the day. His
name was Lucifer, which being interpreted is Son of
the Morning. It was evident that he had not a little
of the waywardness of the fallen angel.

Seated in a light buggy was a man quite as noticeable as the horse. His slouch-hat was tipped back,
revealing a massive forehead. His deep-set eyes were
keen and gray. His nose was sharp His mouth was
large, but well formed, and beneath his thin lips were
exceptionally handsome teeth. His chin was a fine and
strongly marked feature. His head and his thin, almost bloodless face were covered with short, grizzled
hair. His frame was spare and considerably above
medium height. His age was about sixty. He wore
no driving-gloves, and was carelessly dressed in a well-
worn suit of iron gray.

The colt's proud spirit rebelled under the process known as breaking. He had stopped short, to start again only at his own royal will and pleasure. His master sat patiently for a few moments, occasionally saying " Come," in soft, coaxing tones. After speaking several times he got out and, still holding the reins, made a pretense of adjusting a buckle here and there, as though he would impress on the animal that the halt was most opportune. Having done this, he gently stroked and patted him, fondled his head, talked to him, and fed him cubes of white sugar. Then he returned to his buggy and again requested him to move on. This operation was repeated several times without effect. "Come!" said Denman, for the twentieth time. His voice, though calm and low, was growing stern. The soft, coaxing tone had disappeared. In its place was an ominous ring, becoming more and more distinct. Again and again the command was repeated, each time more sternly than before. There was no sign of obedience. Craigin wondered at the man's self-control. Most men with a balky horse, in the most public street of a city, would lose patience much sooner; yet this man again got out, again caressed and fed the animal, and tried to lead him.

"You had better step back," he said to the crowd, when kindness had failed; "you had better step back, or some one may get hurt. Stand back!" he repeated sharply; "I don't want any one hurt."

He kicked the robe under the seat and braced his feet. His fingers tightened round the lines like a vise. There was a dangerous light in his eyes. Drawing a tough, heavy whip, quick and sharp as a flash of light-

ning he struck the stallion a stinging blow on the
flank. A bloody wale followed the lash and left a
stain on the velvety coat. The powerful animal reared
and plunged; but the bit, designed for such occasions
and used at the peril of breaking his jaw, brought him
sharply down. Again and again, keen as a knife, the
terrible lash descended upon his quivering flanks, criss-
crossing them with bloody wales. The brute reared,
backed, plunged from side to side; the man held him
calmly and with consummate skill, all the while punishing him with relentless severity. At length, as the
animal backed suddenly and still more violently, the
wheel cramped and the buggy was upset. Denman
lighted on his feet with the adroitness of a cat; but as
he did so one of the wheels struck his leg between ankle
and knee, laying bare the bone for several inches.

A groan went up from the crowd as they caught a
glimpse of the mangled and bloody limb beneath the
torn garment that covered it; but, beyond a single
oath, Denman uttered no cry. He sprang to the stallion's head and seized the bit with an iron grip. The
muscles in his long, lean hands stood out like cords
of steel. The brute reared and plunged, fought with
feet and jaws. His master hung to him like death.
Several of the boldest of the spectators, Craigin among
them, rushed forward, and the stubborn creature, held
down by many hands, took the punishment that followed without sign of yielding.

"It 's no good licking a balky horse," said Denman,
at length. "Bring that straw," pointing to a crate of
crockery that had just been opened; "we 'll see what
fire 'll do."

The straw was piled under the stallion's belly, and lighted. Fire did not conquer him. He started back with a snort of rage, dragging the men after him, crushing the buggy like an egg-shell against a stone post, nearly catching a bystander in that grim trap. Thus brought to a standstill, he reared to his full height, tearing himself loose even from Denman's grip, and struck at his master's head with both fore feet. The multitude's cry of horror was too tardy a warning. In another instant Denman's career would have been ended, but as the iron hoofs descended a human body hurled itself against him like a thunderbolt, dashing him to the ground just out of harm's way.

He sprang up instantly and seized the bit. The fire had been scattered, and with the help of ready hands the horse was held.

"Mike," he said, "get the grays and a long chain."

In a few moments the grays, harnessed to a beer cart, were driven up. One end of the chain was attached to the rear axle of the cart, and the other was secured around the colt's neck.

Denman turned and grasped the hand of a stranger. "I owe you my life," he said.

Then he addressed himself once more to Mike, the driver. "Start up a little—easy!" His forbearance was not yet wholly exhausted.

The chain was stretched taut. The colt lay back on his haunches and pulled with all his strength.

"Come! get up!" cried Denman, lashing him with the whip.

The infuriated animal plunged forward, made a

vicious attempt to bite, and then, rearing, struck at his master for the second time with both fore feet.

"Mike," exclaimed the latter, springing back, "start those horses d—d sharp!"

Mike obeyed. There was a desperate plunge, a violent struggle, a crackling sound, a groan, a heavy fall. The stallion was dead. His neck was broken.

"Where's the man who saved my life?" inquired Denman, when the tragedy was over.

He had disappeared, and no one in the crowd knew who he was.

VI

"THE PRESENTIMENT IS FALSE"

HE next morning, as Craigin approached the railway station, he saw the man whose life he had saved, and the girl he had met at the great regatta.

"Here he is," cried Denman, springing from his carriage regardless of a bandaged leg, and hastening to meet him.

"I hope you were n't hurt," he said, observing large rents in the young man's clothes, carefully pinned together.

"Not to speak of, only a little cut on my hip," was the reply.

"You put your life in place of mine," continued Denman. "It was a great deal closer shave for you than for me. You 're not going on this train? I want you to come and see us; I want to know you, and I have n't even learned your name. Ah!" glancing at the card given him, "Isabel,—you 've met Isabel,—Isabel, he 's Tom's chum; he 's the Stand-by!"

Isabel's words of thanks were few and simple. Her tone and eyes thanked him most, and told him that

3   33

she cherished the life he had saved immeasurably above her own.

In personal appearance he was quite different from the Craigin she had seen the year before. He had recovered the flesh trained off for the great race and was no longer a gaunt mass of bone and muscle. A heavy growth of chestnut hair, short but curly, adorned the head that had been submitted to the barber's clippers. Tan and freckles had disappeared, and the complexion was a clear, rich blond. The black circles under the eyes were, of course, gone. The husky voice had become clear and musical as a silver bell. He was dressed in a fashionably cut and very becoming suit of Scotch tweed, with necktie to match. The care which he evidently bestowed on such matters made the torn coat and trousers the more noticeable badges of honor, appealing to the girl's heart as scarcely anything else could have done.

"Mr. Craigin, won't you stop over a few days?" pressed Denman. "Won't you? Can't you?"

"Not now," replied Craigin, thanking him. "I must go to Boston on this train, and from there home; but I 'm coming back in a month—I 'm coming here to live."

"Ah!"

There was a slight contraction of the eyebrows, that passed like a flash of light. Craigin saw it, but did not think of it till afterward. There was no awkwardness in the exclamation, unfollowed by comment, for Denman was engaged in assisting Isabel from the carriage and in taking out a traveling-bag and other small articles.

"Here's the train," he said to her, "and here's Tim with the checks. My daughter starts for Newport this morning, Mr. Craigin, to spend a few weeks with the Cliffords."

As the train rumbled into the station, Denman, with a good deal of a limp, led the way to a parlor-car. When the chairs were taken he gave his daughter hearty kisses and pressed a roll of bank-bills into her hand.

"Good-by, Isabel!" he said; "write every day. Good-by, little girl!"

She twined her arms around his neck and returned his kisses with interest.

"You know you're lame, papa," she said, "and you must n't wait till the train starts. Good-by, papa!"

Denman kissed her again, gave Craigin a cordial hand-shake, and limped out. It was touching to see the love that shone in his eyes as he stood by the track looking at her; and there was the same light in her eyes as she sat watching him till the cars left the station.

"Papa hates to have me leave him so," she said at last, turning to Craigin, "that it seems almost wicked for me to go away; but he won't let me stay at home."

As this extraordinary statement did not seem to imply any family unpleasantness, Craigin promptly inquired, "Why not?"

"He says he won't let me sacrifice my happiness to his—as if the happiest times I ever had were n't with papa! You can't imagine how good he has always been to me. As long ago as I can remember he used to romp with me every evening, and then tell me stories till I went to sleep. As I grew older he gave me an hour every night, and we used to read fairy tales and natural-history books together just like two children. I've grown up with papa. Even when he was putting his life into the railroad fight, as you did into the great race, he never was too busy or too anxious to give an hour to his little girl—that's what he always calls me; I shall be his little girl as long as we live. He never spoke an angry word to me in his life.

"I want to show you something," she continued, opening her traveling-bag. "There!" she exclaimed, producing a rich case lined with white satin. "Think of giving those to a girl of eighteen for a birthday present!"

Craigin took the open case from the daintily gloved hand. It contained a pair of diamond ear-drops and a diamond brooch. They were too large and costly—if diamonds are permitted to a young girl—to escape the social law which limits such display before marriage. Without a flaw, limpid as water, brilliant as stars, how they would flash from those perfect ears and on that swelling throat!

"I know girls don't wear such diamonds as those," she said; "but I shall, for papa chose them. It is n't the diamonds I care for,—though I do like diamonds, —it's the love that made him do it."

Why had she shown them? Surely not from vanity; she was proud, not vain. Neither was she a girl to wear her heart upon her sleeve and babble of sacred things to strangers. Her life was in her father, but it was not like her to proclaim it; she was not in the habit of trumpeting his praise. He was John Denman, and well she knew that modesty is the jewel of worth. Why, then, the second time she met him, did she tell Craigin what she would not have told another? Was it because she regarded him as a man apart from and above other men? Was it because she dimly foresaw a war of giants and an agonizing struggle with her own heart?

Beautiful things appealed strongly to the young man, and the admiration he expressed for the gems showed that he knew a good deal about their fine points.

"Your father said you were going to stay at Newport with the Cliffords," he remarked on returning the diamonds.

"Yes; Alice was my chum and classmate at Lake Crescent. We graduated together two weeks ago. That's why I'm on such intimate terms with them; and then, Senator Clifford was one of papa's lawyers in the railroad fight."

"I see by the papers that his doctors have ordered him to go abroad this fall, and that he'll take his family with him."

"Yes; and they've given me the most pressing invitation to go with them."

"Are you going?"

"I don't know. I don't want to leave papa, but he wants me to go. He says it's an opportunity of a lifetime to go with the Cliffords."

"An opportunity to hobnob with royalty?"

"Well, the doors of palaces swing open to Senator Clifford. He's a famous man."

"Of course. He has a European reputation. You've

been abroad once, I know, for I 've heard Tom speak of it."

"I went with papa when I was twelve years old. I have n't been since then."

"A party of two?"

"Mama was with us."

She had been rolling the word "papa" like a sweet morsel under her tongue, had frankly shown that he was her glory and her idol, and her only mention of her mother had been the incidental remark, "Mama was with us." It shed a flood of light on the Denman household, and she saw that Craigin had caught its full significance. It could not be helped, and she quickly turned the conversation to Apsleigh, in the course of which she referred to her companion's engagement with the "Tocsin."

"Why, how did you know that?" he exclaimed. "It is n't out yet. It was n't settled till yesterday afternoon."

"I knew it as soon as you said you were going to live in Apsleigh. So did papa; I saw it in his eyebrows."

"I can't imagine how you knew."

"As easy as one and one and one and one make four—just putting four things together. Tom said you were going to be an editor; you said you were going to live in Apsleigh; I know what kind of a man you are; and I know the other papers would n't have you if you 'd work for nothing."

"So Tom has been talking about me?"

"Yes; he said if you thought a course was right you 'd follow it straight to death and never flinch a hair."

"But he does n't know; I 've never been tried."

"He said lots of other things about you."

"Tom 's a partial witness. He thinks a great deal more of me than I deserve."

"What he said is true."

"You can't know that; you 've never seen me but twice."

"I do know it, not because Tom says so, for I would n't take his judgment altogether where he likes any one as much as he does you; I know it myself."

"How?"

"You 've studied Latin and Greek and conic sections and Porter's Psychology, have n't you?" she inquired, with what appeared to be an abrupt change of subject.

"I 've tried to; I don't know much about them."

"I don't know anything about them. I don't know anything in a scholar's way of knowing things. There's just one thing I can do well: I can read people. Now and then I have to read them bit by bit, as you would pick out hard Latin and Greek, and puzzle over them as you would puzzle over mathematics and psychology; but I can read most people as easily as plain, every-day English."

"I 've often heard Tom speak of it. It 's a wonderful gift. How do you do it?"

"I don't know. I suppose I take it from papa. He 's got more brains in his little finger than I have in my whole head. I can read people better than he can, but he reads them better than any other man I ever saw. At times he 's had a lot of money to invest, and men from far away have come to get him into their enterprises. As long ago as when I was a little girl eight or ten years old, he used to bring them to the house, and hold me on his knee while they talked over their wine and cigars. I did n't understand anything about the business, but I could tell whether they were honest or not."

"Do you mean that he put the judgment of a girl eight years old before Bradstreet, and letters of introduction, and lifelong business reputations?"

"That 's what he did. Seems incredible to you, does n't it? But I told him right. It 's helped him so and pleased him so, I 've made the cultivation of my one gift the work of my life."

"Until you can read men like printed pages?"

"It does n't seem to me any more wonderful, only it is n't so common. The letters of the alphabet tell you all sorts of things and play on all your feelings; and you 're so familiar with them you 're not conscious of noticing them, only the ideas they stand for, are you? If you 'd never heard of a book you 'd say it was impossible, would n't you?"

"Yes; but men have invented the alphabet, and any one can learn how to use it."

"And God has put an alphabet in every man's face. If you had a wicked scheme in your heart you could n't look me in the eyes without my knowing it."

"Do you mean me in particular, or anybody?"

"Well, I confess that was rather personal. A man came to Apsleigh a couple of years ago with a mining scheme. His references and the reports of experts and all were first-class. Papa investigated it as carefully as he could, and told me afterward it looked to him like a straight proposition and as if there were an awful pile of money in it. I was at school, and he wired for me to come home. We had a big dinner. Of course I was the mining man's partner. I made myself as agreeable to him as I could for four hours, and worked the hardest I ever did in my life. He was one of the smartest men I ever met, and his face was the completest mask I ever saw. I don't believe I could have read it if I had n't made him drink so much champagne. The scheme turned out a gigantic fraud. Papa said he 'd have lost hundreds of thousands of dollars if he 'd gone in, and would n't have had his name linked with it for millions, and that I 'd saved him."

"It was hard to read that man?"

"Hard as conic sections."

"And easy to read me?"

"Easy as a-b-c. I 'm going to say an awfully frank, unconventional thing: I 'm sorry you 're going to edit the 'Tocsin.' I 'm almost sorry you 're coming to Apsleigh."

"Why?"

"Because you 're like papa in so many ways, and so different in—in what you call principles."

"I don't like his business, if that 's what you mean," said Craigin, bluntly, almost brutally.

"I don't know as that 's any worse than what I said to you," replied Isabel. "Hundreds of people in Apsleigh don't like papa's business, but they don't dare say so to him or to me. If you were like them I should despise you."

Then they changed the conversation to less personal

matters. When two young people of opposite sex are
pleased with each other there are always plenty of
things to talk about. So it was with the Stand-by and
this strong, brilliant, unconventional girl. There was
Apsleigh, of which Craigin wanted to learn everything, college life, about which Isabel was inquisitive,
boarding-school reminiscences interesting to both,
athletics, Newport—a thousand and one things, little
and big, that came and went, glittered and vanished,
like the ever-varying forms of a kaleidoscope. Was
it incipient love, or merely the buoyant spirits of
youth, that irradiated even the most trivial subjects?
Before they were aware they reached the junction
where both were to change cars. They walked up
and down the platform together till Isabel's train
came, and then parted like old friends.

Plain, honest speech and unconventional ways became the princess of Apsleigh and added greatly to
her charms. Princess she was by the divine right of
beauty and indescribable grace. As Craigin walked
the platform waiting for his own train, he found himself repeating the familiar lines, " Et vera incessu pa-
tuit dea."

When once more on his journey he sat absorbed in
his own reflections, scarcely realizing the direction
they were taking or the consequences they might in-
volve. "If she ever loves," he said to himself, "it will
be a strong man,—strong like her father,—and if she
loves, it will be with her whole soul." Before he knew
it he was dreaming dreams, and awoke with a pain in
his heart.

Without affectation, neither bold nor shy, and grateful for the service rendered her father, the girl had at once, to all appearances, put the young man on the footing most remote from that of a prospective lover—the footing of good comradeship.

What were her thoughts as she sat gazing out the window, unmindful of the admiration she attracted? "I wonder if he knows as much about most things as he does about diamonds? He sees and reads more than he studies, and remembers everything. I never saw a wrist like that before, and his hand is smaller than papa's. Papa and I used to read in the natural-history book that the gorilla's arms are so long and muscular, and his chest and shoulders so huge, that they make him look deformed, and give him strength to strangle a lion or twist a gun-barrel like a wisp of hay. Mr. Craigin is almost like a gorilla, only it's strength without deformity. His smile is the most charming I ever saw, because it comes straight from the heart. He's very distinguished-looking—any amount of brains; a noble, tender heart, and a will like papa's. I wonder if I shall meet a young million-aire at Newport that's fit to tie his shoes? If the viscount were only like him! And yet—no! it can't be true! I won't believe it! He saved papa's life—the presentiment is false!"

VII

BEFORE he had been in Apsleigh a month Craigin wrote a conservative editorial on the liquor question. One evening shortly afterward there was a knock at the door of his sanctum.

"Come in," he said.

A big, burly man entered.

"Be you the new editor?" he inquired.

"Yes, sir. What can I do for you?"

The tone was so hearty and the face so pleasant that the stranger immediately extended a huge, toil-hardened palm, and exclaimed, "N-you kin let me shake yer hand! 'nd you kin print this 'ere in yer paper!" producing a business card.

"Mr. Jones?" said Craigin, glancing at the card, and cordially taking the proffered hand.

"N-yaas; John Rogers Jones, blacksmith, 52 Garland street—that 's me; n-I expec' I wos named fer the man which died with his feet warm. N-I read that piece o' yourn, 'nd I sez ter my ole woman, 'Maria,' sez I, 'I 'd oughter put my sign inter that 'ere "Tocsin" newspaper.' 'Nd here I be a-purpus. Haow much?"

44

"Usual space for a year? Twenty dollars."

"N-I 'm presedunt of the Temp'rance Reform Club," continued Jones, taking a twenty-dollar bill from a fat pocket-book, "'nd I thaot p'r'aps you 'd make us er leetle speech."

"A little speech?"

"N-yaas. N-I hain't a-goin' ter tease yer, 'cos I know you 'll gin us a lift anyhaow. N-I tole Maria, 'Maria,' sez I, 'he 'll make us er darn good speech et the public meetin', 'nd good speeches is scurce es hen's teeth.'"

"I 've heard of the club," said Craigin, filling out a receipt, "but I don't know as much about it as I 'd like to."

"N-I 'll tell you," said Jones, pocketing the receipt and fishing out a brier-wood pipe. "D' you mind smokin'?"

"Smoke all you want to," replied Craigin, handing him some matches.

"N-it makes it kinder easier ter talk. N-eight er ten year back, afore I cum ter taown, one o' the parsons, he 'nd three er four more hot-headed fellers, they went ter prosecutin', 'nd some o' the rummies they sot the meetin'-haouse a-fire. N-that made folks pooty r'arin'. But Denman he drawed his check fer five thousan', 'nd went raound 'mongst the likker men 'nd sez, sez he, ''F you don't help undo what some cussid fools 've bin doin', 't will be laid ter the trade, the whole on 't.' 'Nd so he got five thousan' outer 'm. N-he got fifteen thousan' in all, 'nd it built a new meetin'-haouse, 'nd took the cuss all off, 'nd thare was n't er yap till Jorden 'nd Phelps cum two year ago. N-they

stuck ter what they called morel suashun, 'nd kep' the
pot a-b'ilin' two or three weeks.   N-I 'd jus' cum ter
taown, 'cos I could n't git trusted no more whare I
wos known; n-we wos awful poor.   N-I chawed on 't
er consid'able spell, 'nd then I sez, 'Maria,' sez I, 'I
hain't goin' ter drink no more, never'—n-I hain't,
nuther; n-thare hain't no children cryin' fer bread ter
our haouse naow, 'nd I 've got er good business, 'nd
my debts is paid 'nd munny in the bank.   N-well, 's I
wos sayin', Jorden 'nd Phelps they got up er reform
club, 'nd raised er pile o' munny, 'nd put Dekin Follett
et the head on 't.   N-dekin he would n't spen' er cent,
'nd wanted ter have six prayer-meetin's er week,—
nothin' he likes s' well 's prayer-meetin's, 'cep' figgerin'
int'res',—'nd the club it most petered out.   N-wall, the
riffraff, 's you might call 'em, they put up er job on
the ole man 'nd 'lected Jake Barrus, 'nd Jake he wos
er blasphemin', Tom Paine critter,—wus 'n the dekin,
only t' other way,—'nd he got 'em all sick on 't, 'nd
fooled away the munny, 'nd run the club inter debt.
'Nd then they put in me.   N-I did n't want it, 'cos I
growed up 'n the backwoods 'nd did n't know enough;
but I 've kinder split the diff'rence betwixt dekin 'nd
Jake.   N-anyhaow, the debts is paid 'nd the terbarker-
juice is cleaned up.   Naow we 're goin' ter have public
meetin's once 'n er while, 'nd I 've kinder sot on you
fer the fust one."

"I can't promise without thinking it over," said
Craigin.

When his visitor departed, he paced the floor a long
time thinking it over.   He was beginning to realize
that, for happiness or misery, Isabel Denman was all

the world to him. It was plain that she liked him.
Where was the impassable barrier? He could not
honestly escape voicing the principles of his paper—
even Denman would expect it; but to make public
speeches was beyond his professional duty and the
beginning of more aggressive work. Besides, his ideas
in regard to methods were not settled. Why not
pause to think and study? Why hastily antagonize
the Denmans? Was it a sacrifice of principle to with-
hold his feet from this first step? Love cried, "No,
no, no!" He tried to reason, and in the agony of his
spirit reason seemed to mock him. Then, above the
conflict in his soul, he thought he heard a still, small
voice saying, "Yes." Kneeling on the office floor, he
swore: "I'll live and die doing what I believe is right,
no matter what it costs, so help me God!" Instantly
there streamed into his soul a flood of light that seemed
to come from heaven. "It is my only chance!" he
exclaimed. "She reads hearts, and if I sacrifice my
sense of duty for her, she'll know it and despise me."

When it was known that Craigin was to speak, people—one at a time, fifteen or twenty in all—gave him
hints as to what he should n't say. Last of all came
Deacon Follett also.

"I hope you won't say anything about the law," he
remarked, rubbing his lean chin. "It was kind of
understood when the club was organized. Most of
the liquor-dealers gave something. Mr. Denman gave
five hundred dollars."

"As a sop?"

"N-no—not that—exactly; but, you see, our people
are—conservative. It—won't do."

" Won't do ! " exclaimed Craigin, with a feeling that savored of contempt. " Won't do in free New England to speak of existing laws ! Deacon Follett, we don't live in Russia."

"No; but, you see, our people are conservative— and Mr. Denman gave five hundred dollars."

" The law makes liquor-selling a crime, and provides heavy penalties for officials who do not enforce it," said Craigin, at the close of the interview. " Whisky is sold as openly as flour is. No Republican can advocate a repeal of the law without sacrificing his political future; no man of any party can try to have it enforced without being regarded as a common nuisance, a disturber of the public peace. It 's a queer state of things. I won't say a word about it to-night, Deacon Follett. I want time to study it out."

" Young blood 's so hot," muttered the old usurer, as he walked away. " I was afraid he 'd make a mess of it; but he takes good advice like plum-puddin'."

Craigin's boating record was well known, his adventure with the horse made him noted, and his editorials had attracted much attention. It was already recognized that a strong man had come to Apsleigh. Most of all, however, he was talked about in connection with the Denmans. Everybody was curious to hear him. The hall was filled to overflowing. His stage-fright disappeared after the first sentences. Words came as water flows when the fountains of the great deep are broken up. Back of words were ideas, facts, figures, arguments, conclusions. The lesson pressed home was eradication of drinking tastes by cultivating higher tastes and a nobler life, making the club a reform club in a broader sense than had ever been contemplated.

He knew that he spoke none the worse because Isabel's eyes looked up into his from the crowded hall. In his dreams that night she stood beside him. He stretched forth his arms. An impassable gulf opened between them, widening, widening, ever widening. She vanished forever as two mighty hosts closed in horrible battle. He was leading one, her father the other.

Craigin's speech was an event. From that time he was the real head of the Reform Club. Harmony was restored, the rooms were made attractive, private meetings became informal and pleasant, and now and then an evening was given to simple entertainments, ending with good things to eat. Under the old order members were expected to abstain from whisky, under the new to live clean lives, be honest, pay their debts if they could. As the months went by Craigin shaped and molded the club more and more according to the outlines he had traced. He drew to himself two or three hundred people of the class it was designed to benefit, lifting them to purer lives and nobler aspirations. Among them were women who associated him with sober husbands, happy homes, credit at the grocer's, decent clothes for themselves and their children, who looked upon him as a type of the One who spent his life going about doing good. Among them were men, rough and uncultivated most of them, in whose hearts he kindled the divine flame of love, who would have followed him unquestioningly to death.

4

VIII

ON THE RIVER

"THERE are horses and dogs and guns and boats and fishing-tackle at your service," said Denman. "I keep 'em for my friends, and it 's a great pleasure to me to have 'em used. There 's always a spare knife and fork at our table; drop in as often as you can—breakfast, lunch, or dinner. We all play whist. We want you to come and go just as Tom would if he were living here."

Craigin hesitated, hardly knowing how to express himself without giving offense.

The brewer instantly divined his thought.

"I don't want to compromise you," he continued; "and I promise, if you ever feel called upon to fight my business, I 'll hold you as free to do so as if we were strangers. I like you, and I shall feel more hurt than I can express if you let any scruples of that kind stand between us as friends."

Craigin accepted these hospitalities in the spirit, though not to the extent, they were offered, and his intimacy with Denman himself was a source of great pleasure. Even before Isabel's return from Newport he saw clearly why father and daughter were all the world to each other. Isabel inherited her father's brains and her mother's beauty. But Mrs. Denman was blessed with considerable tact and more indolence. A late breakfast in bed, an elaborate toilet, embroidery when she felt industrious, a light novel when she did not, lunch, a siesta, a bath, a more elaborate toilet, a drive, a call or two, dinner, and whist—this was her daily routine. As to the establishment, Denman kept a competent housekeeper. The wife and mother had no cares, and was as contented, as amiable, and as purely ornamental as a petted pussy. She was still extraordinarily beautiful, and had the faculty of saying little and appearing to be intelligent. Denman kept open house. United States senators, governors, congressmen, brewers, liquor-dealers, traders, horsemen, and plain Yankee farmers put their legs under his sumptuous but democratic mahogany. The conversation, from Gladstone's policy to the fine points of a horse, was almost always good of its kind, and Isabel, even when a little child, generally understood it far better than did the beautiful woman, whose tact, combined with her husband's pride, rarely permitted her to betray her ignorance.

Denman sent Isabel to a fashionable boarding-school at an early age, because she was practically motherless and his company was almost exclusively masculine. For the same reasons he was glad to have her spend her vacations with the Cliffords and get an opportunity to mingle with the best European society.

Denman's grounds, almost a park in extent, sloped back to the Apsleigh River.

One October afternoon Craigin came up from the landing.

"I 've bought a shell," he said, as Isabel met him in the hall, "and have called to see if you 'll join me in trying it."

"With the greatest pleasure," she replied. "If you 'll excuse me, I 'll be ready in a few minutes."

As she went to her room she recalled a remark she had made weeks before and had not thought of since. It was: "I 've always been accustomed to boats and rowing, but I never was in a shell, and should like nothing better than to try one."

"I 'm sure he bought it for me," she said to herself.

She soon returned, having exchanged her afternoon dress of golden-brown silk with velvet trimmings of a darker shade for a boating-suit of soft white flannel —full skirt, blouse waist, and cap—adorned with anchors embroidered in old-gold floss-silk.

"You 're the only girl of my acquaintance I 'd dare take out in a shell," observed Craigin, as they started out together.

"The only one you 'd dare drown?"

"The only one I would n't be afraid of drowning, for it 's as easily upset as a birch-bark canoe."

"So 's my own boat—almost."

"Yes; I did n't dare ask you till I had tried it. I knew if you could manage that, you could balance a shell."

"When did you try it?"

"Oh, I took that liberty a good while ago."

The answer satisfied Isabel that the shell was bought on her account.

"What a beauty!" she exclaimed as they reached the landing.

It was indeed a beauty—a first-class Spanish cedar Elliott, long, light as paper, slender as an arrow; made, like a greyhound, for speed alone.

"Beg pardon! but the crew must go aboard to receive the passenger," said Craigin, laying the boat alongside the little wharf, and taking the rower's seat. "There! now I 'll hold it steady for you."

When she was seated and the motion had died away, he gently pushed off an oar's length from shore. His first strokes barely stirred the water, and meanwhile she watched closely every motion. The delicate craft, trimmed almost to a feather's weight, glided along without a tremor.

"Our cockswain himself could n't beat you!" he exclaimed at last, falling into a long, easy, regular sweep, that indicated perfect confidence. Straight away up the river they sped, mile after mile, the athlete at the oars, the girl at the rudder.

"Now let me row!" she cried as they neared the rapids and turned the bow homeward.

"I don't dare."

"I won't upset it, and if I do, I can swim like a duck."

"Ducks are n't handicapped that way," he replied, with an admiring glance at the costume, which strikingly set off her dark and splendid beauty, but was not at all adapted for swimming.

"You can swim, can't you?" she inquired.

"Yes."

"Then there can't be any danger."

4*

"But a crab may mean getting wet."

"I 'm not afraid of water, and I won't catch crabs."

He pulled up to a log and exchanged places. The rolling seat cost her a crab or two, for the motion was new to her; but she quickly became accustomed to it, and was delighted with the power it gave. The forests were robed in all the glories of Indian summer, and the river rolled slowly on in its majesty, gleaming in the sunlight, black in the shadow, unruffled by a breeze. The girl was in the mood for testing her skill and strength to the uttermost. There was something almost fierce in her energy, yet none of it was wasted. It was like the action of a thoroughbred horse, that trots to the point of breaking and never breaks. The shell sped on faster and faster. Each stroke left its graceful swirl farther and still farther behind. Craigin sat in the stern and watched the rower, divine in the grace of motion, her glorious features flushed with health, glowing with exercise, sparkling with exhilaration. He caught also a glimpse of something more —the spirit of the moment.

Suddenly she rested the oars and sat motionless and silent.

"I 've learned something in spite of boarding-school!" she exclaimed at last. "I can row and swim and skate and ride a horse—ladylike accomplishments, are n't they? I was n't such a very bad scholar, either; I graduated fifth in my class."

"And I only fifteenth," remarked Craigin.

"Fifteenth in a class of two hundred is better than fifth in a class of nine, is n't it?" she replied. "Any-

how, what difference does it make? I wish I'd been
a man and had lived twenty-five years ago!"

"Why?"

"Because there was life worth living then, and
death worth dying."

"Not more then than now."

"What do you mean?"

"That men must live and die to save the republic,
as they did twenty-five years ago."

"I know what you mean, for I heard your speech
the other night. You mean the liquor business."

"Yes; that and other things—that most of all."

"You really mean what you said, that it had done
more harm to English-speaking people than war and
famine and pestilence combined?"

"That's what Gladstone says. I believe it's true.
The nation could stand it well enough if the evil were
confined to drunkards themselves, but that's the smallest part of it."

"What did you mean by saying men must die?"

"Something very different from what you were
thinking of. Not death at the cannon's mouth, a
nation's praise, a hero's name in song and story;
that—"

"That's a death brave men covet," interrupted Isabel.

"I meant a living death, fighting for God and the
manhood of men; misunderstood, jeered at as a crank,
disowned by one's dearest friends, cut off from honors
and advancement, isolated, reviled, hated, persecuted,
belied."

"That's a death only the bravest can face."

"Thousands and tens of thousands must face it,"

replied Craigin. "Do you know how the Turks took Constantinople?"

"No."

"There was a deep trench in front of the walls. When they had made a breach in the walls, men flung themselves into the trench until it was full, and horse, foot, and artillery passed over them to victory."

"How horrible—and heroic!"

"In great reforms myriads of men must fling themselves into living graves for the world to pass over them to higher things. In one way or another, human progress is over bleeding hearts. It always has been so; it always will be so."

For several minutes not a word was spoken. Suddenly there was a splash. A muskrat had dived from the river bank. The boat had drifted close to the shore.

"If he thought a course were right," said Isabel to herself, "he'd follow it straight to death—that kind of death—and never flinch a hair. He's a hero if there ever was one! And papa—the terrible fight—. the presentiment! I won't believe it—not yet!"

What she said to the hero was quite different from what she said to herself. "Don't you think it's your turn to row now? I'll pull up to that boom, and we'll change seats."

When once more seated in the stern she introduced a momentous question: "I'm to have a new traveling-hat, and there are two at the house that are just too lovely for anything. Mama and I can't tell which we like the better. I'll leave the choice to you."

IX

WHEREIN DANIELS DIFFER

A T almost any time within twenty years the liquor interest might have reported, "All is quiet in Apsleigh." A quick ear could now catch mutterings of a rising storm. The Reform Club had acquired influence and position. The "Tocsin" was gradually assuming a more aggressive tone. There was much agitation elsewhere, and men began to ask one another if something could not be done in Apsleigh. A temperance "union" was formed. It included people of all shades of opinion, from Eben Harpswell to people who drew the line at getting drunk and selling to sots. This motley organization began its career with a vast amount of talk. Agreeing in nothing else, it finally agreed to vest its powers and responsibilities in an executive committee, upon which its members, with astonishing unanimity, declined to serve. At length the twenty gentlemen whose names stood first on the call, of whom ten were clergymen, were conscripted, and were authorized to do battle on the implied basis of "Heads we win, tails you lose."

After many meetings the committee decided to ask the city fathers to do what the law commanded and their oaths of office required. A petition was circulated. Some signed because they wanted the law enforced, more because they favored closing two or three low dives, hundreds as a joke "to see the mayor and aldermen wiggle," and the great majority because they were asked to and it cost them nothing. The city fathers talked the petition over from week to week, and received many intimations from influential members of the Temperance Union that a fight with Denman was not to be thought of. They were told that nearly every one, except Harpswell and his small following, would be satisfied if Bridget Maloney and One-legged Gibbs were attended to. In due course of time the old woman and the cripple retired from mercantile pursuits and took refuge in the almshouse. Three aldermen made themselves politically unavailable by declaring that it was cowardly to prosecute two paupers and let a millionaire sell barrels where they had sold pints. The mayor and six aldermen protested that prudence was not cowardice. They said it would be better to go slowly and make thorough work of it. They made thorough work of going slowly. Months passed and nothing further was attempted. The "Tocsin" published sarcastic and stinging editorials. A local Junius dipped his pen in gall. The executive committee demanded that something should be done. Mass-meetings were held. Prosecuting members of the city government for criminal neglect of duty was publicly discussed.

As the official year wore on the clamor died away

and interest centered upon the next election. The contest was sharp, and the mayor and his six liquor colleagues were returned by a handsome majority. There was a fly in the ointment. At each of the caucuses a resolution had been introduced instructing the candidates, if elected, to enforce all laws of the State so far as they were required to do so by statute and official oaths. Objections to resolutions so worded could hardly be made, and a free-whisky government was elected on a prohibition platform. It was not elected by anything like a strict party vote. It was scarcely inaugurated before the demand for consistent action became louder than ever. The five or six men of peace on the executive committee had dropped out, and the others were united and plucky. They waited on the city fathers.

"Here is the law," said their chairman, opening a book that lay on the table. "It is violated thousands of times a day within gunshot of this council-chamber, and you know it. Here is the statute requiring you to enforce it, and making you liable to criminal prosecution if you don't. Here are the instructions under which you were elected, directing you to enforce all laws so far as your official duty extends. I myself heard you take your oaths to do so. Do you intend to keep them or to violate them?"

"This has been an—extraordinary—and—painful—interview," said the mayor when the committee had withdrawn. "The—situation is—embarrassing—very—and—perhaps we had better—take counsel."

The city solicitor was summoned.

"I don't believe in prohibition," he said; "I believe

in license, and know most of you do; but that's neither here nor there. The statute is plain as day. You have n't any choice in the matter."

"There 'll be the devil to pay if we go for John Denman," remarked one of the aldermen.

"There 'll be the devil to pay anyway," was the comforting reply. "You 're caught between the upper and nether millstones, and they 'll grind you to powder."

"Looks—that—way," wailed the mayor.

"Yes; you 've got the army blue on, and it 's only a question of being shot fighting or being shot trying to dodge."

"We—don't—want—to—dodge," groaned the mayor, "and—we—don't want to be—shot—either."

His fat chin fell upon his chest, and great beads of sweat stood on his brow. He seemed to shrink and dwindle bodily, as if his portly figure were much too conspicuous a target.

"Would—you—feel—hurt—if we should—call in other—counsel?" he inquired at last, piteously.

"Hurt! Should be delighted! It 's for you to say whether to prosecute in behalf of the city, and if you say prosecute, I won't sacrifice my honor by shirking what the law puts on me; but I tell you, I don't hanker after any part of it."

He was dismissed, and Mr. Woods, Denman's professional adviser, was called in.

"Unfortunately," said Woods, "we have a sumptuary law, and its enforcement is primarily committed to you. In so unpleasant a matter, of course you don't wish to exceed your duty?"

"No," replied the mayor, promptly.

"But, as honest men, to do your duty, neither more nor less?"

"Y-yes," said the mayor, unconsciously shaking his head.

"I'm sorry to have to differ from my learned young brother, your official counsel; but it's an old legal maxim that reason is the life of law, and even statutes must be construed and enforced according to common sense. The statute says you shall prosecute every person guilty, and so forth. Literally that means any person in the State. Have you the right to go from county to county prosecuting at the expense of Apsleigh? Even Dr. Bradford would n't claim it means what it says. What does it mean? It says you shall prosecute if you can obtain reasonable proof. In a sense I can take a trip around the world; in another I can't, for I can't afford the time and money. In a sense you can sacrifice your business and turn spies; as language is commonly used—and the law makes that the rule in construing statutes—you can't. It's no part of your duty. It is n't what you were elected to do."

"Mr. Woods," inquired an alderman,—he was a new member who had not been considered dangerous,—"Mr. Woods, if men were murdered in this city as openly as liquor is sold, if the statute made it our duty to prosecute, and if we should fold our hands and say we can't get evidence, what do you suppose the community would do?"

"It's against the law," replied Woods, "to drive faster than a walk over Denman Bridge. It is n't three hours since I saw the chairman of this over-righteous committee violate that law. If there's no difference between little things and big, why don't you prosecute the Rev. Dr. Bradford?"

"Is n't that a matter which the law leaves to our discretion? Does it say we shall prosecute? Have we taken any oath to do so?"

"Well, it's pretty much the same with the prohibitory law, in spite of the 'shall' and the oath. There's a statute authorizing city councils to regulate the sale of liquors and the places where they are sold. That cuts prohibition as soap cuts grease, does n't it? Amounts to a confession that it can't be enforced in cities, does n't it? You've spoken of murder, Mr. Capen. What would you think of a statute making it a capital offense side by side with another authorizing city councils to regulate its commission and the hours and places in which it may be committed?"

"Which is the older," inquired Capen, "the prohibitory law or the law authorizing regulation?"

"I don't know."

"If the prohibitory law is the more recent, would n't it in effect repeal the other?"

"These ordinances exist in every city in the State," replied Woods, evading the question.

"Have n't been set up as defenses to liquor prosecutions, have they?" persisted Capen. "Whatever the law says city councils 'may' do, it says the mayor and aldermen 'shall' prosecute, does n't it? Puts that in our oath of office, does n't it? Makes us liable to criminal prosecution ourselves if we don't, does n't it?"

"Suppose it does? To be required to prosecute, you must have reasonable proof."

"That is n't what the statute says, Mr. Woods. It says 'can obtain.' Are n't liquors sold as openly in this city as groceries are?"

"What of it? Reasonable proof is proof that gives reasonable assurance of conviction. Men will leave the State before they 'll testify in liquor cases. They 'll lie on the witness-stand when they 'd tell the truth about anything else if it cost them thousands of dollars. Grand juries won't indict, and petty juries won't convict, no matter how strong the evidence is."

"As bad as that?"

"I don't call it bad. It 's just as it ought to be. When it was death to steal a shilling, when it was imprisonment and mutilation to tell the truth about men in office, English juries redeemed English humanity and English liberty by putting common justice and common sense before their oaths, and all the world honors them for it. Why not say what we all know? The prohibitory law is such a meddlesome and outrageous interference with personal liberty that it 's impossible to enforce it in a free country. It never was intended as anything but a sop to cranks. It was understood that they were to have the law, and the people the whisky. The Republican party has n't a vote to spare. If a few hundred cranks should refuse to vote the ticket without a law against kissing, members of the legislature would tumble over each other in their haste to pass the law, and boys and girls would kiss more than ever. Do you think those same members of the legislature, if they were on a jury, would let a fine young fellow be sent to jail for kissing his girl?"

"Do you mean," interrupted Capen, "that if we don't like the law we should disobey it and violate our oaths?"

"The voters of this State don't want such oaths kept, and take good care not to elect men who will keep them. You 're the servants, not the masters, of the people, are n't you? They want the law for political reasons only. They won't have it enforced. I 'll put it on this ground, if you like it better: the wicked prejudice against the law, if you choose to call it so, is an important fact to be taken into account in deciding what is the reasonable proof on which you are required to act, that is, what proof is reasonably sure to convict. It 's an old maxim that the law does n't demand impossibilities of anybody, not even of the mayor and aldermen. If it should command you to dip up the Atlantic Ocean with a quart pot, you would n't be bound to do it, would you?"

"What—would—you—advise?" asked the mayor, raising his head, with a sigh.

"You might authorize the city marshal, as chief of police, to enforce the law, and instruct him to enforce the ordinances."

"Authorized to enforce the law, and instructed to regulate its violation!" exclaimed Capen, when the vote had been taken. "If we don't have the contempt of honest men on both sides, it won't be because we have n't earned it!"

X

RAIGIN published the particulars of that session. He wrote editorials so biting and caustic that they were copied far and wide, even by journals that had no sympathy with prohibition; and far and wide people shook their sides over the torment of the Apsleigh city fathers and in imagination "saw 'em wiggle." Every one laughed at them. Some despised them. No one hated them. They had avoided making enemies, and in the lottery of politics they might soon be again "available" as "prudent and conservative men."

Events took a different course. At a recent session of the legislature an act had been passed declaring that all buildings, places, and tenements used for the illegal sale, or keeping for sale, of intoxicating liquors were common nuisances, and might be enjoined or abated as such upon the petition of twenty or more legal voters. The legislature, occupied with a great railroad fight, passed the act without thought or discussion. When it adjourned people discovered, or thought they did, that the new law was an irresistible

5   65

engine of warfare. Hope and fear, a desire to exalt or condemn the law, ignorance of legal principles, and sensational journalism combined to set the wildest ideas afloat. Many imagined that the liquor traffic could be abolished by petitioning the Supreme Court, and even intelligent men supposed that an injunction would be a perpetual encumbrance on real estate. Armed, as they thought, with such a tremendous weapon, advocates of prohibition became zealous for war. For a time their confidence and the demoralization of the enemy made their imaginary advantage real. In a number of the cities and large towns petitions under the nuisance act were sharply followed by prosecutions under the old law, and many liquor-dealers, bewildered and disheartened, made the best terms they could, and were enjoined by consent. Apsleigh alone had a Denman, and, while the war of words went on, there seemed no disposition to come to blows.

Weeks had passed into months when, one morning in May, Eben Harpswell entered the county attorney's office. If Harpswell had lived in the days of the Inquisition he would have gloried equally in going to the stake himself and in sending others there for the slightest differences of opinion. He was a man of small caliber and great activity, utterly incapable of comparing means with ends, sincere, narrow, fanatical.

"Mr. Strickland," he said, "I want you to enforce the nuisance act. Here are the papers."

His manner was that of one claiming the right to command and expecting it would be questioned. It was the lawyer's first intimation of the proceedings.

He controlled his impulse to swear, lighted his customary sedative, and mechanically read the papers from beginning to end.

"What evidence have you got?" he inquired at last.

"I 've got twenty names. What 's the need of evidence?"

"I can't do anything without evidence," replied Strickland, his voice trembling with indignation.

"I don't see why not. The law says 'upon petition of twenty or more legal voters.' It does n't say anything about evidence."

"Another law," exclaimed Strickland, "says that on petition of one person a dangerous lunatic may be sent to the madhouse! Do you think that means without proof that he 's a dangerous lunatic?"

"Then how 's the new law any better than the old?"

"I don't know that it is. It has n't been tried."

"Has n't been tried! Have n't you read a newspaper for two months?"

"Is a battle-ship tried before any one knows whether her guns are steel or solder?"

"Well, if the new law has n't been tried, it 's high time it was. I want you to go right ahead with those papers. You can get evidence enough."

Strickland refilled his pipe and smoked in silence, fighting hard for self-control, while his visitor eyed him suspiciously.

"Mr. Harpswell," he said at length, "John Brown tried to free four million slaves with a dozen men and as many old muskets. His heart was right, but his head was wrong. It 's the same with you."

"I 've only done what 's been done in other places."

"Done in other places! In other places the movement was led by influential men of all political parties, evidence was collected beforehand, court was in session instead of five months away, and there was no John Denman. Even in those places it remains to be seen whether it's anything more than a passing whirlwind. It's different here. How you got three or four of those names I can't imagine. They won't train with you, and the rest will damn the movement in public opinion from the start. You've begun war without a cartridge, or a gun to fire one in. You withdrew from the Temperance Union, publicly declaring that it had n't the courage of its convictions, and would n't do anything, and never intended to do anything. The members of its executive committee, whom you despised as cowards, have a glimmering idea of what war with Denman means, and are quietly preparing for it. You have cut off their only chance of victory."

"I had no idea—"

"Of course you had n't! If you had ideas, as many as Denman, and were as squarely on the other side, you could n't do a tenth of the mischief you've done already. The war has got to begin now, not because you say so, but because you've gone so far it can't be helped. These signers can't hold their tongues a couple of months."

That evening, after a hard day's work, Strickland sat in a cheerful room, in anything but a cheerful frame of mind. He had scarcely eaten since breakfast.

"What's the matter, darling?" asked his wife, smoothing his forehead with two white hands, and kissing it in a pretty way she had.

He drew her upon his knee and kissed her. Then he held her from him, so he could watch her face, and said, "Bessie, how would you like to leave Apsleigh?"

"Leave Apsleigh! Why, Mark, what do you mean?"

"Just what I say, dear. How would you like to leave Apsleigh?"

"What is the trouble, darling?" she said, kissing him again. "It must be something dreadful. Have you lost your money?"

"No; it is n't money. There 's going to be a liquor war." He told her all about it. "I 've had a great deal to enjoy and look forward to in Apsleigh," he said, "but when this is over I shall have nothing. I shall be ruined politically and professionally, half my old friends will be enemies, and as to staying here, I 'd rather be in my grave."

"Could n't you resign?"

"On the eve of battle?"

"O Mark, I 'd rather see you dead than dishonored! But it won't be as bad as you think. You don't care so very much about politics, do you? And if it hurts your business—you say Wilcox makes more money selling mortgages and things than you do practising law: you might do something of that sort."

"Throw up the finest profession in the world and turn mortgage-broker! No, Bessie; we 'll go West and start again."

"I 'll go, Mark, when the time comes, but it won't come. You have n't brought it about; you 're only where the law puts you; and they 'll think all the more of you for doing your duty." Then she added, with a woman's inconsequence: "They won't do anything dreadful,—burn the house or try to kill you,— will they?"

"I wish they would!"

"O Mark!"

"The house is insured, and I'd as soon they'd kill me as not. 'T would n't be half as bad as what's before me. I believe in prohibition where it's possible —if it ever is. I'd be willing to die to make it win, and killing me would raise a storm of public indignation that would make it win. There's no hope of anything of that kind. If there are Harpswells in Denman's camp, he'll make 'em curl like whipped hounds."

"Mark, what makes you so bitter against Harpswell? He means well."

"I know it."

"And Denman does n't. He's a bad man."

"No, Bessie; he is n't a bad man. He's a giant on the wrong side."

"What's the difference, Mark?"

"All the difference in the world. There never was a worse cause than the slaveholders' rebellion, and the men who fought for it were just like those on our side. Their greatest general was the finest kind of a man. Denman's got more good in him than fifty common men, though he won't scruple at anything to win this fight. I could bear defeat from him, but to be ruined by a fool in our own camp—it's unbearable!"

"If you should want to go, Mark, I'll gladly go anywhere in the world with you, anywhere you think best. There's no place I can't be happy in with you and our boy."

"I know it, Bessie, and it is n't so much ourselves I care about—though I do want to keep this house for our boy, because it was his great-grandfather's—I don't care as much about ourselves as I do about the party."

"Why, Mark!"

"We have n't any votes to spare. I 'm afraid it 'll give the State to the Democrats."

"Suppose it does, Mark? What of it?"

"Bessie!"

"I know you 're the best husband that ever was, and I know how you love us both; but it hurts me, Mark—it seems awful to hear you say you care more for the party than for yourself and me and our little boy. I can't understand how any one can feel that way."

"Bessie, you 're a Christian if there ever was one."

"I try to be a Christian, Mark. Why?"

"And you believe in the church of Christ?"

"More than in anything else; more even than in you, darling."

"Bessie, I believe in the Republican party as you believe in the church; it 's my religion."

"O Mark! I know you don't mean anything of the kind; but that seems almost like sacrilege to me."

"It is n't sacrilege, Bessie; it is my faith, like your faith in the Christian church. I believe in God; I believe he has chosen our country to be the Moses of the nations, and there 's only one party in it fit for a divine mission. It 's through that party that government of the people, by the people, and for the people has not perished from the earth. It 's the hope of the future for this nation and for all nations. I believe the Republican party is God's instrument. More than any other, I believe, it is founded on Christ's teachings."

"You must n't blame me, Mark, if I can't see anything divine in politics,—I 'm only a woman,—but, darling, if the Republican party has God's purpose to work out, you won't defeat it by doing what the law makes it your duty to do, even if it does look as if it might give the next election to the Democrats."

XI

ISABEL went abroad the November following Craigin's arrival in Apsleigh. During
her absence he wrote to her occasionally,
and received replies at irregular intervals,
written in her frank, unconventional way.   In one of
her letters she said: "I have met Mr. Gladstone, and
have dined with the Prince of Wales.   I mention these
events in the order of their importance."   At another
time she wrote: "I have had a great honor for an
American girl and a plebeian—a chance to marry an
echo of bygone centuries.   Hundreds of years ago a
knight with a few companions held a narrow pass
against a mighty host until the king and his army
came, and the kingdom was saved from invasion.
Then he sank to the ground covered with wounds, and
as his life-blood ebbed away the king laid his sword
upon him and made him a count.   And his descen-
dant, the present count, can waltz like a dancing-master,
and play the fiddle; and he—this dancing, fiddling
carpet-noble—told me of his great ancestor to induce
me to marry him.   What do you think I told him?
I told him if he would take me to the cathedral where

the bones of his great ancestor are buried, I would marry the bones."

She returned from foreign lands about six months before the Harpswell affair. Her dark and splendid beauty had grown more dazzling than ever. It was such as her mother's had been at twenty, with a litheness of form, a strength and activity of body, and a grace of motion that the indolent belle, Miss Isabel Andrews, had never possessed. She had cultivated her special gift more than anything else, and among statesmen and princes. Craigin knew she could read the love in his heart, although she never appeared conscious of it. Sometimes he half believed she loved him in return, but of that she gave no sign. Their relations of good comradeship were stopped from going further by an indefinable barrier, as if each felt the shadow of coming events.

One Thursday afternoon, one of his quarter-holidays, Craigin took his gun and started for Ash Swamp. There had been a fresh fall of snow, and although it was not the most favorable time of day, he hoped to bag a brace of partridges or a rabbit. In passing the Denman mansion he saw Isabel coming down the walk, and waiting for her at the gate a pair of superb, milk-white horses attached to a single-seated, high-backed Russian sleigh, with silver-tip bear robes and silver screen.

"What a magnificent turnout!" he exclaimed.

"Is n't it lovely?" replied Isabel. "It 's a Christmas present from papa—only it is n't Christmas yet. He said Santa Claus ought to come with the snow. I 'm going to try it for the first time. Grace Wyman was going with me, but she 's telephoned that she has company and can't. I shall have to go alone—unless you 've nothing better to do for an hour?"

Thus ended the rabbit hunt.

The conversation drifted to life in great English country houses.

"I 'd rather be an earl than President of the United States," said Isabel, as she finished her description of an earl's life.

"Why, I thought you a marvel of democracy for a young lady who 's been chaperoned by the Cliffords in the courts of Europe."

"I 'm not," she protested emphatically. "I 'd believe in a nobility, eldest son and all, if I did n't believe a hundred times more in *noblesse oblige*. Americans pretend to despise what they have n't got, and envy and worship it in some one else. If they can go back seventy-five years to a stupid side judge they plume themselves on their birth, and would make fun of my waiting-maid for giving herself airs with our cook, just as a Vere de Vere would make fun of them. Perhaps it 's all absurd, from Vere de Veres down, but I 'd rather be absurd than a hypocrite. I 'll venture to say half the English aristocracy don't care as much for blood as I do, and I 'm every inch an American girl."

"What makes you care so much for it?"

"For the same reason that people would want whisky ten times as much as they do now if they could n't get it—because it 's the one thing money can't buy or brains win."

"But you thought more of meeting Gladstone than of dining with the Prince of Wales?"

"Yes; Gladstone is—Gladstone, and the prince, if it were n't for the accident of birth, would be a common man."

"The French count had family enough, had n't he?"

"He was the eleventh count in direct line."

"And you despised him?"

"Yes."

"Yet you say you care a great deal for family—for blood?"

"Yes, I do; but—let me show you! Come, ponies, show the stuff you 're made of!"

The road was level as a turnpike, the sleighing superb. The colts, covering the ground with flying feet, held their speed like veterans, their mistress handling them with the skill of a trainer.

"Blood or not, they 're trotters from forelock to pastern!" she exclaimed at length, checking them, and glowing with pride. "Do you think I don't prize them more because they come of famous stock? But what if Thunderbolt should carry himself like a scrub, and claim the honors of the Derby just because his great-great-great-grandmother won it? He has a pedigree and does n't disgrace it."

"I see what you mean," said Craigin. "A man is one who does great things; family is a line of men."

"That 's just it," replied Isabel. "The old count who held the pass was a man. If his blood had kept its virtue I 'd have bowed down and worshiped it; but eleven generations had turned it to water."

"Blood to water, and land to air!" mused Craigin, half to himself and half aloud.

Isabel turned on him with flashing eyes. "Do you think I despise a man because he 's poor?" she cried. "The count was rich,—one of the richest men in his province,—but he was a coward. A boat upset; he swam ashore, and left ladies to save themselves as best they could."

"And had the presumption to propose to you after that?"

"Do you think I 'd have let the creature speak to me after that? But I knew what he was before. I know a coward when I see one."

In the course of the winter the "Big Six" gave a ball. A Big Six ball meant the best music in Boston, the best people (from a society point of view) for forty miles around, a deal of dress, much pleasure on the part of those within the charmed circle, much envy on the part of those without—in a word, it was the social event of a winter in Apsleigh. Craigin went with the Denmans, and as they sat together at a corner of the banquet-table they could not help overhearing a conversation just outside, for the door had been left ajar, and the young men spoke louder than they realized.

"She 's the handsomest girl I ever saw," said one of them.

"My sister 'll be wild about that white satin and the diamonds," said the other.

"What are diamonds and Worth dresses to Isabel Denman?" exclaimed the first speaker. "She 'd be the belle of the ball just the same in a calico gown."

"What 's she going to do?" queried the second speaker. "Marry Craigin or the new Earl of Throckmorton?"

"Marry Craigin—I'll bet you fifty dollars she does."

"All right. I'll bet fifty on the earl. If she don't have either, it's a stand-off."

"They say the earl's handsome, and an awfully good fellow, and blue-blooded for a thousand years. Isabel Denman would like a pedigree and a coronet as much as anybody; but I tell you, Frank, she loves Craigin, and an emperor could n't get her away from him—if he does n't get into a fight with the old man."

"Fred, there won't be any fight. Craigin can't do anything alone, and he's the only man in this city that's got the sand to stand right up to John Denman and give and take to a finish."

"Yes; and the old man'll have to be prodded mighty hard before he'll turn on a young fellow that saved his life."

"It's kind of queer, though, to read his paper, growing ranker and ranker every week, and see him round with the Denmans the way he is!"

"That's why I bet on him. Do you remember the circus chap who was here last summer?"

"The one who did n't wear tights or chalk his soles, and rode six horses bareback, smoking and talking and laughing as if it was n't any more of a trick than falling off a log?"

"Yes. It was n't so much the things he did as the way he did 'em. Here's Craigin carrying himself the same way—captivates everybody, no one can quite tell how. Denman despises a coward and worships a hero, and Isabel's a chip of the old block. They don't like what he's doing, but they like him all the better for having the sand to do it. I tell you, it's going to beat the earl; he is n't in the race."

Of the four listeners Mrs. Denman alone showed the embarrassment they all felt. Craigin would have given all he had to read Isabel's thoughts as she read his; but that he could not do.

PART TWO

THE FIRST CAMPAIGN

I

THE day and the hour came. The city clock struck nine. The hostilities precipitated by Harpswell began. The high sheriff, seven deputies, and twenty-three assistants left convenient loitering-places and started, according to previous agreement, for their respective scenes of visitation. In five minutes it was generally known that something unusual was taking place; in ten that the long-talked-of liquor war had begun. Groups of excited people stood about watching the officers, wondering who had signed the complaints, whether they would dare meddle with Denman, what he would do if they did, and how it all would end. The drug stores were not molested; the raid was confined to other places where liquor was sold. At most of them not a drop was found. Such was the case at each of Denman's hotels. His wholesale warehouse, however, contained hundreds of barrels. The secret had leaked, but there had not been time to remove so large a stock.

Notwithstanding the substantial failure of the search, the dealers were notified to appear before the

83

police court on the following morning, and not far from a hundred witnesses, taken almost haphazard, were summoned. At the appointed time the proceedings were adjourned to the county court-house, and even that large building was packed to suffocation with all sorts and conditions of people. One by one the defendants pleaded not guilty, waived examination, and gave bail. The strangest thing was their good humor. The spectacle of a great organization like the Temperance Union, and the executive committee with its brave speeches, abandoning the field to Harpswell was ludicrous, and, in spite of the dreaded nuisance act, the movement was already known as the Cranks' War.

There were those who did not laugh. "Mr. Strickland," said one of them, "this is none of our work; we wash our hands of it."

"Dr. Bradford," was the reply, "I wish you 'd step up to my office."

The conference was a long one.

"This war is n't of my seeking," said Strickland. "I 've never believed in getting too far ahead of public opinion. But that 's neither here nor there. It 's come. Harpswell 's a fool, and deserves a fool's fate; but, all the same, the only honorable course is to fight. If we back out now, every temperance man in Apsleigh has got to hunt his hole and stay in it till he dies."

That night the active members of the executive committee held a protracted session, and unanimously voted to enlist for the war. It had been declared, and preparation for it was yet to be made. The city government and city marshal were hostile. Most of the

local leaders in politics were either hostile or waiting
to go with the majority, though a few were friendly
after the manner of Nicodemus, secretly and by night.
The wealth and influence of the city were, as it was
commonly put, "conservative." The Temperance
Union was in fact the Temperance Disunion. Half
the executive committee were clergymen, whose practical wisdom was a subject of lay incredulity. Then
there was Harpswell, an object of terror to his friends
and of hope to his foes.

In Denman's storehouse, under a keeper, were some
forty thousand dollars' worth of liquors, every drop of
which was liable to confiscation. The executive committee proceeded to take the bull by the horns. The
process *in rem*, that is, against the liquors themselves,
was new to Strickland; for in twenty years it had been
resorted to scarcely a dozen times in all the State.
He drew the papers as best he could, and every active
member of the executive committee signed and swore
to them. The service of these papers was the first intimation that an enemy very different from Harpswell
had entered the field.

Denman occasionally lost his temper. From his
standpoint, he never before had such great provoca-
tion. Within ten minutes after the warrant was served
a pair of grays attached to a beer wagon dashed down
Main street, turned the corner of Garland street, and
tore up to his storehouse at full speed. Denman
sprang to the ground before they stopped. Upon a pile
of barrels sat the sheriff's keeper, a brawny giant, two
hundred and fifty pounds of bone and muscle, motionless as a graven image, grim and silent as a Roman

6*

gladiator, and withal a man of known courage. For a moment Denman glared at him without speaking; then he seized a barrel of Medford rum by the chimes, tipped it over, and rolled it to the door.

"Here, Jim," he said, "take hold! Fly round sharp!"

He was thrust aside, and the barrel was rolled back and set on end.

"Mr. Denman," said the keeper, "these liquors are in my charge. You must let them alone."

"In your charge? And who are you?" cried the owner, with an oath.

"Usually," was the calm reply, "I 'm only Dick Spaulding, but"—unconsciously quoting a great king —"to-day I 'm the State."

"Jim," said Denman, after bestowing a fervent curse on Dick Spaulding, and the State too, "Jim, call the boys! Get every truckman you can! We 'll have these liquors, State or no State! Tell 'em I 'll pay 'em and stand by 'em."

"Mr. Denman," interposed Spaulding, drawing himself up to his full height of six feet two, and looking the magnate of Apsleigh squarely in the face, "if you get these liquors, you 'll get them over my dead body, and it won't be the only dead body, either. I 'm put here to keep these liquors, and I shall do it. Mark Strickland says the law 'll bear me out in it, life or death."

"Well, then, it 's death, for I 'll have 'em!"

"Mr. Denman," said Woods, appearing at the doorway, "it won't do!"

"What won't do? Here 's forty thousand dollars'

worth of liquor gone to hell! I don't care for the money, but—" The air was thick with profanity.

Gnashing his teeth, he hastened away, and met his pastor at the corner of Main street. "See here!" he snarled, "I gave twenty thousand dollars to build your church! I subscribed half your salary! I 've paid the last cent I ever shall, and, what 's more, your stay in this town 'll be short! You 're a fine specimen of gratitude—meddling with my business! You 're a Christian, you are."

"Mr. Denman," replied the clergyman, "I have interfered because your business interferes with mine."

With a parting curse Denman rushed on, sprang up a stairway, and burst into Strickland's office.

"Have you made out papers for the seizure of my goods?" he demanded.

"I have."

"What are you going to do with them?"

"Have them condemned if necessary."

"No, you won't! They 're worth forty thousand dollars."

"I can't help it if they 're worth forty millions."

"Well,"—with a torrent of maledictions,—"I 'll see about that! I 'll have those liquors!"

"No, you won't!"

"I 'd like to know why?"

"Because they 'll be defended with powder and lead if necessary."

"I don't care a d— for powder and lead!"

"You might for prison-bars, and that 's what it would come to. Mr. Denman, I wish you well; don't try it."

"Wish me well! Who and what are you, to wish me well or ill?"

He descended the stairway, leaving imprecations behind him. An hour later he was himself again — a quiet, self-contained man of fertile brain and iron will, preparing for such a fight as no one in Apsleigh yet dreamed of.

"It's a great day for Apsleigh!" exclaimed Harpswell to a group of men who were watching the transportation of Denman's liquors to a county building.

"It was a great day for Charleston," replied one of them, "when Sumter was bombarded."

II

THE LOCKOUT

THERE was a gathering on Apsleigh Avenue in the evening of the "great day for Apsleigh." According to society standards the company was not select. Neither was it festive, although the table was laden with fruits, wines, liquors, and cigars. Occasionally there was a bitter laugh, but curses were more frequent. In a more important respect than profanity and refreshments, the meeting was strikingly unlike those of the executive committee: there all held equal rank; here, by common consent, one man was dictator.

"It's war," said Denman, calmly and grimly, as the conference ended, "and war means money. Money and public sentiment together are irresistible. We have one; we'll have the other. Harpswell has already won us half the battle. There must be no demonstration, no insult to any one, no outrage of any kind. The burning of another church would be our ruin. If I don't sell in the State, the law can't touch my brewery; it will coin money for the fight. Besides, the help are our friends, and I would n't shut down and let 'em suffer, anyway. The nuisance act can't be enforced if I retire from business in my other places. I have retired. To-morrow morning every guest and permanent boarder in my hotels will be notified to leave. Next day at noon the houses will be closed. My friends of the other hotels and the restaurants will gladly do likewise. We 'll stand together and lick these cranks, horse, foot, and dragoons, till there is n't a grease spot left of 'em."

The Sunday after the hotels closed there was a mass-meeting in the city hall. Harpswell was there in high feather, and many others in feather not so high. Dr. Bradford made the opening speech, a plain statement of what the executive committee hoped to accomplish, and an earnest appeal for support. Craigin followed with a masterly ten minutes' talk. He asserted that no wrong had been so monstrous that, at some time in the past, it had not been sanctioned as inalienable right. "The divine right of kings," he said, "the right to sit in place of God and judge of other men's beliefs, the right of private vengeance, of private war, of slavery—all these have been unquestioned by the world. Where are they now?" He spoke of how the race is fighting its way steadily up to the golden age, the age of the future, not the past. "We are the Moses of the nations," so he claimed, "and the fulfilment of our God-appointed leadership depends less on blood and iron than on the virtue of our citizens." Then, in a few words, he told how the abuse of liquor makes for pauperism, disease, ignorance, degradation, vice, and crime, for all vile things, all things corrupting politics, all things that sap the nation's life. "A generation ago," he said, "the South defied the law of the land. Men said it could not be enforced. Business was disorganized. Government bonds were wildcat investments. Billions of dollars were thrown into a pit that seemed bottomless. Hundreds of thousands of brave men went to death; hundreds of thousands more took their places. Righteous law was enforced. Treason was suppressed, and in suppressing it slavery was blotted out. From waste and agony and death have come justice, peace, prosperity, a recreated nation. Through all the ages men will thank God for the grandeur and the glory of the great uprising which saved government of the people, by the people, for the people, to the peoples of the earth. There is coming yet another great uprising. Righteous law must be,—and must be enforced. We must work out our destiny. The perils of the future must be met and done to death like treason and slavery. It can be done. Brave men can do it." Then he closed with an appeal to stand firm at all costs—an appeal so earnest, so impassioned, it made that great audience for the moment kindred spirits with himself.

Closing the hotels had aroused the people. Severe comments on Denman's course were well received from unexpected sources, and in response to a call, and on a canvass made before the meeting broke up, many persons consented to open their houses to the traveling public. Arrangements were made for publishing a directory of such houses, and delegates were chosen to see that strangers were cared for on the arrival of every train. The results of political and personal dislike for Harpswell were in great measure counteracted by the stand of the executive committee. The audacity of an attack on Denman captivated the multitude. The meeting closed with great enthusiasm. The leaders were surprised and encouraged. At that time volunteers were abundant, but, as in '61, powder and shot, rifle and cannon, were wanting.

Weeks passed. All saloons and bar-rooms were closed. Drunkenness disappeared. The city was orderly beyond precedent. Some regarded the war as ended, and were astonished that what had seemed so difficult had proved so easy; others knew it had scarcely begun. In the absence of stirring events the business outlook became the chief topic of newspaper discussion. All of the papers published interviews. Stanch temperance men claimed that local trade in the necessaries and comforts of life was increasing. No one could deny that business from other places was falling off with alarming rapidity. The crusading spirit gradually fizzled away, like gas from soda-water, while the shadow of the giant grew larger. Forbearance under prosecution, or, as many put it, persecution, and the extraordinary quiet and good order, won over, as Denman had foreseen, influential people whom anything like an outrage would have made allies of the executive committee. It became irksome to entertain the traveling public. Strangers disliked the restraint of private houses and the consciousness of being unwelcome guests. Everybody who could shunned the town. Rival towns took advantage of the situation. Apsleigh was losing touch with the business world, was in danger of becoming isolated and decayed. Those who at first thought

Denman had made a mistake in closing the hotels began to look at it differently, and the reasons which he gave for doing so in great measure transferred the odium to the other side. Shortly after the hotels closed he went away—"to see about investments elsewhere." He did not return until the tide had begun to set strongly his way. The next morning a "Times" reporter found him at his office, to all appearance as free from anxiety as if no rumor of trouble had ever reached his ears.

"I called to interview you in regard to the hotels, if you 've no objection," said the reporter.

"Not the slightest. Won't you have a cigar? I 've closed the houses because I don't want to run them at a heavy loss."

"It 's made a great stir."

"Of course. How do you like that cigar?"

"Best I ever smoked."

"Then you 'll do me a favor by taking the box. Clifford has a plantation a few miles west of Havana, —best tobacco land on the island, best in the world,— and he 's sent me a whole case."

"Really, Mr. Denman," exclaimed the reporter, greatly flattered, "I don't think I ought to accept such a present! They 're so choice and—"

"Don't mention it!" interrupted Denman. "I can't get any more of Clifford, for he won't take pay; but I 've arranged to buy of his agent, and shall have the pleasure of treating my friends to what they can't find outside of Cuba."

"It 's a snap to be one of your friends. But I must finish this interview and write it up for the type-setters this afternoon. Perhaps I 'm trespassing on your time ? "

" Not at all," said Denman, to whom the interview was of great importance.

" You say you have closed your hotels because you can't run them according to law without loss ? "

" Solely for that reason."

" The bar receipts must have been very large ? Excuse me for asking the question, Mr. Denman. I would n't have you think—"

" I 'm glad you asked it. When it 's given out that the hotels are closed because they can't be run in conformity to law, and the reasons are not explained, people take it for granted, as you did, that the bar trade is a substantial part of the income. My hotels would pay handsomely without selling a drop, if I could only hold the custom."

" Which means that most people who travel want a good deal of liquid refreshment, and won't go where it is n't to be had ? "

" Not at all. Most of my guests drink very little, and many of them nothing. It costs about as much to run a train half full of passengers as if it were crowded, does n't it ? "

" I should think so."

" And the receipts are only half as large. It 's much the same with a hotel. Whether it 's full or half full does n't make twenty per cent. difference in expenses, and it makes a hundred per cent. difference in receipts. Take the Apsleighshire House. With two hundred guests the gross receipts are about eight hundred dollars a day, and the net profits about two hundred. With only a hundred guests the daily receipts are about four hundred dollars, and the expenses about four hundred and eighty. There 's nothing for me to do but shut up my houses."

"I see."

"Most people away from home like a glass of wine or beer at the table when they feel like it, or a nightcap when they go to bed. Whether they care much for it or not, they resent being refused, and go away mad and talk against the house. It 's human nature. Then, every one 's especially liable to ailments away from home, and wants to feel that he can get a little whisky or something of that kind without calling in a doctor he does n't know. There 's another class—an important one: nine tenths of the men and women who never drink won't patronize a temperance house."

"Why not?"

"Because a house that 's full can afford to set a good table and have everything up to date, and a house that is n't can't. People who don't drink are as fond of good things to eat as anybody is, and expect as much for their money."

"I 'm sure of that, Mr. Denman. I 've reported all sorts of banquets, and know that for eating the parsons take the cake."

"You 'll notice," continued Denman, "that the estimates I 've given, in supposing the hundred guests spend half as much as the two hundred, leave bar receipts entirely out of account. As a rule, people who spend money for drink spend for other extras, and there 's a big margin of profit in all kinds of extras. Of course I don't deny that the bar receipts are quite an item; but they alone don't cut much figure in the difference between a handsome profit and a heavy loss."

"Yes; I see now just how it is."

"Of course you do. I 've been in the hotel business twenty-five years, and think I know as much about it as the ministers do. It would cost several thousand dollars a month more to run my houses according to law than it would to let them stand idle; that 's why I closed them."

"Mr. Denman," said the reporter, "if people had understood this matter, they would n't have blamed you."

"Of course they would n't. No one can expect me to throw money away."

"I shall want to make a very careful report of this interview," continued the "Times" man. "I will show it to you for correction."

"I wish you would. By the way, when those cigars are gone, you 'll know where to find more of the same kind."

Denman's reputation for truth was good. He was too honest to lie, except as a war measure, and too shrewd to lie and be caught. His statement had immense weight with the public. The "Tocsin" did not accept it as altogether true and commented on it severely.

III

"I SHALL HATE YOU"

APSLEIGHSHIRE people already talked about Craigin, as they long had about Denman, as every one talks about noted statesmen, generals, and pugilists. He still frequented the house on Apsleigh Avenue. As the speaker behind the door had said, the old man was disposed to bear a great deal of prodding before turning on the young fellow who had saved his life. His good will was not yet changed to hate, and his respect increased as his good will diminished.

"To publish what he did to-day, and sit here with Isabel and wife and me playing whist, like one of the family—it's the coolest thing I ever saw!" said the old brewer to himself. He was so lost in admiration that he lost the trick.

Isabel, Grace Wyman, Mr. Hobbs, Grace's lover, and Craigin played lawn-tennis together one afternoon not quite two months after the closing of the hotels. When refreshments were served Miss Wyman and Mr. Hobbs not unnaturally found themselves at one end of the tennis-court, and Isabel and Craigin at the other.

"We 've been good friends a long time, have n't we?" said Isabel, putting down her plate, and abruptly changing the topic of conversation.

"Yes," replied Craigin; "three years, counting from the boat-race."

"It seems such a pity we must be enemies! I 'm more sorry than I can tell, but it can't be helped."

"Can't be helped?"

"You think your course is right and won't flinch a hair, and this is hardly the beginning. Papa 's thought the world of you, in spite of all you 've said and done; but it can't last much longer. He 'll hate you pretty soon; then I shall hate you too."

Her bearing was proud and firm, but her bosom swelled, and Craigin thought he heard a faint sound like the choking back of a sob.

"Hate me, right or wrong?" he said.

"Yes; right or wrong."

"Right or wrong?" repeated Craigin.

"Papa's friends shall be my friends, and his enemies my enemies, right or wrong. I wanted to say this," she continued before he could answer, "because there 's another thing I must say before it 's too late. It 's this: I know there is n't anything cowardly or dishonorable about you, and when papa and I hate you, we 'll give you good, square, honest hate. One can't hate an enemy one despises."

"I 'm sure—" began Craigin.

She interrupted him with a question. "Do you believe in presentiments?"

"I don't know. Why?"

"I do. I can't account for them—not entirely. All I know is, mine come to pass. Two years ago, when you first came to Apsleigh, I had a presentiment that you and papa would be enemies; it's never left me. I would n't believe it, because you had saved papa's life—and because I did n't want to; but it's coming true. There's going to be a terrible fight. It won't end this year, perhaps not next—and papa 'll break you."

"Is that last a presentiment too?"

"Are you stronger than the railroad company was? It tried to crush papa. Where is it now? In his box at the bank."

"Suppose he does break me? what of it? Men must be broken, and hearts too, that right may triumph."

Isabel looked him full in the face, and after glancing at the couple who had forgotten everything but each other, said solemnly: "It is n't right! It's wrong! It's wicked! It's worse than wicked; it's *mean!* I don't like the liquor business—that is n't it —I hate it—but—have you ever read about the massacre of St. Bartholomew?"

"Yes."

"The Huguenots and Catholics were living together, just the same as people lived together here before you came, trading, visiting, marrying, making money, having a good time, when all at once, at the tolling of a great bell, the Catholics turned on the Huguenots and cut their throats, men, women, and little children. Was that a fair way to put down heresy?"

"No; it was n't."

"It 's the way people are treating papa. He 's been selling whisky and making beer ever since I was born. They 've encouraged him to put hundreds of thousands of dollars into the business; they 've said what a fine thing it was for Apsleigh to have it in the hands of a man who could regulate it as he has; and they 've stood, hat in hand, begging for his money. They 've got it, ministers and all, for their Reform Club, for their churches, for everything they call good—more than any other ten men in town have given; to poor folks, that needed kind words and a helping hand, more than any other hundred men have given; and now they say it 's blood-money, and are trying to rob him of it. Ever since I can remember it 's been nothing but praises of papa. He 's had all he could do to refuse the honors they wanted to give him. They 'd have made him governor, member of Congress, United States senator, if he 'd only consented; and now he 's John Denman, the criminal, and they 're snarling at his heels like a pack of curs round a lion. Why did n't they do as you did—let him understand in the first place that they did n't like his business and would crush it out if they could? Because they did n't dare to. That 's why papa and I respect you and despise them. That 's why I say papa 'll break you—because they 'll run away by and by, like the cowards they are, and leave you alone. I shall stand with papa to the end. I 'd fight them if I were he. I hate the business, but I 'd fight them just the same. There! I 've said what I wanted to!" A touch of her father's iron will half repressed the tremor of her voice as she

added, " I 'm glad it 's said, for we sha'n't be on speaking terms much longer. Now let 's beat Mr. Hobbs
and Grace."

Craigin stayed to dinner and played a rubber of
whist, after which Denman, for the first time, introduced the subject on which they differed so widely.

" Do you know," he said, " that the new Unitarian
church was built to promote crime ? "

" Why, no ! " replied Craigin. " But I understand
you gave twenty thousand dollars toward building it."

" Yes; to promote the crimes perpetrated there
every Sunday. You and your minister and Henry
Harnett, and a lot more of the law-and-order people
of this city, are liable to fine and imprisonment for
blasphemy. There 's one of the old blue-laws left
over in this State, entitled ' An Act to Prevent Blasphemy,' that makes it a crime to deny the divinity of
Christ. What would all you Unitarians do if you
should be prosecuted as criminals for worshiping God
decently, according to the dictates of your own con-
sciences ? "

" We 'd say the law is an outrage against human
rights. We 'd appeal to the constitutional guaranties
of religious liberty."

" Suppose the courts should take the same position
they have in regard to certain other rights ? Suppose
they should say, ' It is n't a question of religious liberty
at all. Fear of hell-fire keeps the masses from vice
and crime. Unitarians don't believe in hell-fire, and
so they 're dangerous to public morals, to good government, to the very existence of free institutions, and
must be suppressed. It 's a matter clearly within the

7*

police power of the State, for self-preservation is the first law of States.'"

"Then we'd say that all men are endowed by their Creator with certain inalienable rights; that higher than any finite court or law or constitution is the primary, eternal, and inalienable right of man to think for himself on the great questions of God and immortality, and to speak his convictions with decent regard for the rights and feelings of others."

"Which would be defying the law?"

"Yes."

"Resisting it by force, if necessary?"

"Yes; if there were a fighting chance of success."

"You mean that it would justify taking up arms, killing people, bringing on civil war?"

"Yes; all the horrors of a religious war if there were a fighting chance of success, not useless, hopeless bloodshed and misery."

"That would be rebellion—treason?"

"Yes, technically, if it failed; revolution if it succeeded; a patriotic duty in either case." .

"Well," said Denman, "you're the squarest man I know. You've seen all the time what I was driving at, and have n't hedged a bit. Your position in this matter is mine on the liquor question. This old law, that's been on the statute-book for a couple of hundred years, has been used once since I can remember to quiet a loud, foul-mouthed blasphemer who shocked everybody; but only a fanatic would dream of enforcing it against those who express religious opinions in a decent way. The people of this State would n't stand such an outrage twenty-four hours. The prohibitory law answers a like purpose. It does well enough to shut up low dives, to keep men from selling to drunkards and children; but the fact that one man in a hundred eats too much pie or drinks too much beer does n't give the State a moral right to take pie or beer away from the other ninety-nine. I know the courts in this State say it 's within the police power, the same as the courts of the Inquisition said religious opinions were; but higher than any finite court or law or constitution is the primary, eternal, and inalienable right of man to eat and drink in moderation, with decent regard for the rights and feelings of others. There are tens of thousands of better men than I am, men who have no pecuniary interests at stake, who believe, as I do, that a prohibitory law is such an outrageous and intolerable meddling with personal liberty that anything necessary to resist it is justifiable."

"I think I understand how you look at it, Mr. Denman. I 've never doubted your sincerity."

"And I 've never doubted yours. I 'm sure I 'd feel just the same if I had n't a dollar at stake; but I was induced to invest hundreds of thousands on the general understanding that the law was only intended to prevent abuses, and I 've always done all I could to keep the business respectable. I had a hard struggle at first, but for twenty-five years 'most everything I 've touched has turned to gold, and I could lose the money I 've got tied up in this business without feeling it. I don't care much about the money, but I won't be robbed of it. I think I 've a right to act as the Unitarians of this State would act if they were prosecuted for their religious opinions. I respect you more than I do 'most any one I know; we 've been good friends; I owe you my life; and I want to tell you fair and plain that if this thing goes on I sha'n't shrink from necessary war measures. I 'm outside the pale of the law, and of course you 'll understand that, if I were to be bound by what you might consider fair fighting, I 'd be helpless. It 's only ten o'clock, and I guess the cook 's fixing something nice to eat; let 's have another rubber to get up an appetite."

When Craigin went home, two hours later, Isabel bade him good night with a steady voice. As soon as he was gone the proud girl flung herself on her bed and burst into uncontrollable sobs.

"It 's the last time," she moaned, "the last time we shall ever meet as friends. It killed Harry, and now —it 'll break his heart and mine!"

IV

THE TEETH OF THE LAW

THE executive committee held many sessions during the two months of quiet that followed the seizure of Denman's liquors. Strickland was often called. In the beginning he had said he would attend if sent for, and not otherwise. He dwelt constantly on the necessity for evidence. The sum and substance of his counsel was, how to get it.

"I don't want to hire detectives, if I can help it," he said. "They 're expensive, and I don't like 'em. We can't count on topers; they all lie. If they tell the truth, a jury won't believe 'em. It is n't my duty to go hunting for evidence, and I won't do it. There 's a good deal to be had without hunting. The internal-revenue collector's books are evidence against those who have paid the United States tax, and they all have. The books of the freight offices will show the transportation of liquors in barrels, to whom delivered, and when. The truckmen, if they don't lie, will furnish evidence of the same kind. The records of the express office will show the delivery of the more ex-

pensive liquors, that come in smaller packages. All
the employees at the saloons, and most of the employees and permanent guests at the hotels, have seen
the law violated daily. Some of them will tell the
truth. Bars and bar fixtures were found at all of the
places. Denman had forty thousand dollars' worth
of liquors on hand. It is n't reasonable to suppose he
had all that for private use. All this and more can
be had without much hunting."

"I should think it ought to be enough," remarked
Dr. Bradford.

"We want the cases so strong," replied Strickland,
"that a jury can't say 'Not guilty' without perjury
plain as sunlight. Systematic work will make 'em so.
Every business man knows enough to hang half the
dealers in town, if it were murder instead of liquor-
selling. If you ask 'em about it, they 're dumb as
oysters, but among themselves they talk. The liquor
men are talking all the time. Denman talks. He
pitched into one of you about meddling with his business,—an admission of guilt,—and he 's been inter-
viewed by the press. One thing leads to another—a
rill to a brook, a brook to a river, a river to an ocean.
There 's no limit to the evidence that half a dozen
shrewd, quiet men can accumulate in a few weeks."

From a carefully prepared list of thirty names half
a dozen men were selected, the fidelity, discretion, and
opportunities of each being a subject of anxious debate. Some were men of social position; not one
would have done detective work for pay. The work
given them did not interfere with their ordinary business. It was to keep their ears open, note down every

night what they had heard during the day, together with time, place, circumstances, and the names of all present, and report to Strickland once a week. At first their notes were enormous in quantity and almost worthless in quality, for they had no idea of what was legal evidence and what was not; but instruction set them right, and before six weeks had elapsed the results far exceeded expectations. It was no light task to systematize evidence collected in this way; but under Strickland's supervision the executive committee did it thoroughly. Thirty-nine little books were written, one for each defendant or firm. Each contained the names of the witnesses in the order in which it was expected they would testify. Under each name was an abstract of the evidence which it was expected the witness would give. Every book was carefully indexed for instant reference. The list of witnesses, numbering several hundred, was mainly taken from the respectable classes, and included a large sprinkling of the élite of Apsleigh—women as well as men. At the same time another little book was in process of compilation—a digest of judicial decisions and authorities bearing upon all questions liable to arise.

At length Strickland stopped crying for more evidence. "Four of the defendants," he said, "have left the State for good. Against all but one or two of the rest we 've got such a mass of testimony as I believe was never yet laid before a jury in a liquor case. If this work had been done to begin with—if it had n't been for Harpswell—I think we 'd stand a chance to win the fight."

"Don't you think so now?" exclaimed several at once.

"No; people believe the city will be ruined. Property-owners are scared to death; business men are afraid of bankruptcy, working-men of hunger, and patriotic men of hurting the Republican party. They won't pull together in anything as they used to do. Their hands are against their neighbors, and there's hate in their hearts. All this is laid at our doors. Public sentiment is turning against us. Denman is growing stronger every day. A political campaign is at hand. The Democrats will declare for a license law. Republicans are all at sixes and sevens. The term of court will be just before election, and nothing can keep politics out of the jury-room. We're beaten sure as death, unless you dare—"

"Dare what?" exclaimed Dr. Bradford, as Strickland paused and scanned the faces of the listening group.

"Dare cut loose from precedent and fight Denman as he'll fight you. It's the only chance of victory. I've been thinking it over for a couple of months, and looking up the decisions for a hundred years back. The principle is established. I can't see why it should n't be applied to liquor cases as well as to other cases. I've made up my mind that the teeth of the prohibitory law have never yet been shown."

"What do you mean?" cried the committee, almost as one man.

"I mean this," replied Strickland: "that each day for a year back on which a man has been a common seller of spirituous liquors he has committed a distinct offense, for which he may be fined one hundred dollars and be imprisoned six months; that each day for a year back on which the same man has kept spirituous liquors for sale he has committed another distinct offense, for which he may be fined fifty dollars; that each day for a year back on which the same man has kept malt liquors, wine, or cider for sale he has committed still another distinct offense, for which he may be fined ten dollars; that each sale of spirituous liquors for a year back is still another distinct offense, punishable by a fine of fifty dollars; that each sale of malt liquors, wine, or cider for a year back is still another distinct offense, punishable by a fine of ten dollars; and that on each offense laid after conviction of a prior offense the penalty may be increased from two to fivefold. Furthermore, that on each offense charged the man may be held to furnish bail in the sum of not less than two hundred, and not more than four hundred, dollars. Leaving individual sales and what are known as subsequent offenses entirely out of account, a man may, in possible contemplation of law, if my position is sound, be imprisoned for a good deal more than one hundred years, be fined tens of thousands of dollars, and be held to bail in several hundred thousands. The liquor traffic has practically ceased for the past two months. The next term of court, from which the statute of limitation would date, is three months away. This disposes of five months. As to the other seven, those books on the table cover every day, Sundays excepted."

"This looks pretty savage!" exclaimed one of the committee.

"It is savage," replied Strickland. "It 's war. You know what Sherman said: 'War 's hell, and the more it 's hell the sooner it 's over.' There are two ways of carrying it on: McClellan's way, and Grant's way—make-believe, and the real thing."

"You propose to fine these rumsellers fifty thousand dollars each, and shut them up for life; is that it?" inquired the Methodist member.

"Not if I can help it. I don't want any one fined or imprisoned. My idea is to let them choose between surrender on such conditions that they can be clapped right into jail if they go into the business again, and taking their chances with the law as the court may hold it, and the evidence piled on that table a foot deep."

"Do you think Denman will surrender?" inquired Dr. Bradford.

"Denman surrender!" exclaimed Strickland. "Not while the world stands! But the rest will have to, and the decks will be cleared for the fight."

"This is a matter to be slept on," said Dr. Bradford. "I move we adjourn till to-morrow evening."

On the following evening the committee assembled with unusual promptness, but no one seemed in haste to take up the question they had met to decide.

"I did n't like Strickland's slur on McClellan," remarked the only Democrat on the committee. "McClellan was a loyal man and a better general than Grant. It 's strange how politics blinds men!"

"Strickland is unreasonable in his prejudices," remarked the Rev. Francis Pemberton, whose allegiance to the Republican party was wavering, and who was classed as doubtful in the canvass. "He believes in prohibition, and has ten times the feeling against a third-party Prohibitionist that he has against a rumseller."

"So have I!" exclaimed the Hon. Silas Bean, who was given to a plainness of speech that was often embarrassing. "The rumseller only fights for his own interests, and the third-party man stabs his friends in the back."

"Gentlemen, I think it is time to call this meeting to order," said Dr. Bradford, suddenly convinced of the fact by the turn the conversation was taking.

After some debate, the committee decided to adopt Strickland's suggestions. They sent for him, and spent the night in arranging details. About a week later a truckman brought some large boxes to the residence of one of their number, and they began to hold protracted sessions there. These sessions were peculiar. There was no debate and little conversation. As many members as could sat at a large table, and the rest sat at smaller tables near by. Each was armed with a pen. On one end of the large table was a pile of printed blanks. A seal had been affixed to each blank, and on each a certain month and day of the month had been written in three places. This work had been done by two young ladies who could keep a secret, and who were spending ten hours a day up-stairs in preparing more blanks. The member nearest the pile took a blank, wrote his name on it, and passed it along. His neighbor signed it, and passed it along. Thus it went from man to man until it bore the names of all the active members of the committee. This process continued several hours at a time and several days in succession. Occasionally, when Strickland dropped in, the members held up their right hands and swore that what they had signed was, in their belief, true. Then Strickland wrote his name in two places on each blank. After he had signed them, a young lady folded them and made them up into little packages with rubber bands around them. On the back of each blank was a printed formula, showing, among other things, the exact nature of the charge, and against whom made. For example, there were three packages labeled "October" on which Denman's name was printed: one containing complaints charging him with being a common seller, another with keeping spirituous liquors for sale, and a third with keeping malt liquors for sale. Each package contained one complaint for each week-day in the month. There were like packages against thirty-four other individuals and firms, and November was a repetition of October, and so on for seven months. In all there were about seven hundred packages and about eighteen thousand complaints. The manual labor of writing one's name so many times was no trifle, and every now and then a member would get up, stretch his legs, and rub his stiff fingers.

"Have you any idea," asked the Rev. Chauncey Watkins, at one of the first of these sessions; "that a tenth of these papers will be used?"

"No," replied Strickland; "I have n't."

"Then what 's the use of having so many?"

"If we have them, we sha'n't use them; if we don't have them, we shall be beaten for want of them. Our only chance is to be overwhelmingly prepared at every point."

"But most of these men can't stand fifty complaints. There 's O'Leary; he can't stand ten. What 's the need of five hundred?"

"Mr. Watkins," said Strickland, "what makes Denman the power he is?"

"Why, I suppose it 's his money and brains and courage."

"Yes, and one thing more, Mr. Watkins: he never goes back on any one who stands by him. He won't leave his old guard to die alone, as Napoleon did at Waterloo. He would n't do such a thing for a throne, and men will die for a man like that. If there 's a chance to save his friends, he 'll take it; if there is n't, he 'll tell 'em to make their peace and leave him to fight it out alone."

"So you think," observed Watkins, "that O'Leary means Denman?"

"Yes; and even Denman can't bear up under eighteen thousand prosecutions."

"I hope they have n't any idea of what we 're doing," said Dr. Bradford. "When Mrs. Skidmore went through the hall awhile ago the door was open, and she saw the papers piled up on the floor."

"Well, doctor," said the Unitarian minister, giving his clerical brother a sly poke, "it 'll be as long as eternal punishment before they guess."

"Doctor," said Strickland, as the meeting broke up, "I want to smoke before going home; won't you come into my office and look on?"

"I wish Craigin was a little older," remarked Bradford, accepting the invitation. "He 'd be our Denman."

8

"He's 'most as old as Napoleon was when he crossed the Alps, older than Pitt was when he became prime minister," replied Strickland. "Before this thing ends —God knows how, I don't—we'll all be following his lead, as the liquor men follow Denman. We'd be as crazy as Harpswell, doing what we are now, if it were n't for his paper. We could n't make it understood, and we'd go down in a storm of public indignation."

"As far as I can make out," said Bradford, "neither you nor Craigin think what we're doing now is going to end the war?"

"Craigin does n't. I would n't want it known, for it would discourage some of the others. He thinks we've got to lose the first campaign."

"Why does he think so?"

"Because that fool Harpswell made delay ruin, and we had to begin before we were ready."

"You say you've got all the law and all the evidence you want?"

"Yes; I'm looking to next term of court. That's as far as I can see. Craigin's got a longer head than I have. He's looking 'way into the future. His plan is to mold and fuse the temperance sentiment of this county into one solid mass, to make temperance men an army instead of a mob, to enlist on our side every human motive, from pure philanthropy to greed of gain and office. It seemed like a chimera to me when he first spoke of it, but he's studying it out day and night in all its details, and he believes it can be done."

V

PROSECUTIONS EXTRAORDINARY

HE complaints measured fifteen bushels and weighed half a ton. The battle was opened by serving notice on each defendant and summoning witnesses for the following day. Hundreds of people, indignant at being summoned in liquor cases, found themselves among the élite of the town, who wondered what they were wanted for. The court-house was crowded. Even standing-room was hard to get.

"I present a complaint against Mr. Denman," said Strickland.

It charged Denman with being a common seller of spirituous liquors on the day before the date of the Harpswell prosecution. The names of the signers created a sensation.

"Mr. Denman will plead not guilty, waive examination, and furnish bail," said his counsel.

"I have another against Mr. O'Leary," continued Strickland.

Complaints against thirty-five different parties were disposed of in the same manner. Strickland took them from his coat pocket, and thus far the defense had no intimation that more were coming.

"Here is a second complaint against Mr. Denman." And he resorted to another pocket. It was exactly like the first, except that the offense was laid on the preceding day.

"Let me see that complaint!" exclaimed Woods. "What does this mean?" he demanded, on looking at it.

"What does what mean?"

"Two complaints for the same alleged offense. Everything printed. Nothing in writing but dates and signatures. How many of these things are there?"

"In all, or against Mr. Denman?"

"Either—both."

"Between five and six hundred against Mr. Denman; about eighteen thousand in all."

A perceptible thrill ran through the court-room. Men and women looked at Strickland and at each other in blank amazement. Some of the defendants turned pale. Denman, always pale, betrayed no sign of emotion, except that his teeth were set.

"Eighteen thousand!" Woods cried. "Preposterous! Monstrous! Impossible!"

"I may as well state my position at once," Strickland said. He did so in the midst of a death-like silence. Then he gave the authorities on which he relied, reading slowly from his little book, and waiting for the judge and the counsel to take minutes of volume and page.

"Suppose the law is as you claim, and suppose you persist in this outrage, where's the evidence to

maintain eighteen thousand prosecutions?" demanded
Woods.

"Here," replied Strickland, pointing to thirty-five
large, thin books beside him; "here, and from this
cloud of witnesses. I want you to have time to inves-
tigate the law. I want these defendants to understand
my position. I don't want any of them fined or imprisoned, but simply that the lockout which is ruining
the town may be ended and the law obeyed."

"So you make opening the hotels a condition of
royal mercy," sneered Woods.

"No; the law has nothing to do with closing the
hotels and systematic diversion of business to other
towns. You can judge as well as I can whether self-
interest will change all this when it is understood that
the law must be obeyed. If you'd like these matters
continued until to-morrow—"

"I think it would be well," interrupted the judge.
"I want to examine the law myself."

Judge Bond was not in sympathy with the liquor
traffic, but, like hundreds of other good men, he was
strongly opposed to the methods which Strickland
and the executive committee had adopted. He was a
good lawyer. He was also incorruptible, conscientious,
and impartial, and everybody knew it. He adjourned
court, determined to know, if possible, what the law
was. He hunted up all authorities within reach, read
them carefully, some of them several times, and then,
lighting his pipe, tried to consider, analyze, and weigh
them from all points of view.

Under the decisions it was clear that one might be
guilty as a common seller, as a keeper of spirituous

8*

liquors, and as a keeper of malt liquors all on the same day. The question was whether he could be guilty of each of these three distinct offenses on each day for an indefinite period. No court, so far as he could find, had ever decided that question. The principle, however, had been applied time out of mind to common-law nuisances. Was there—could there be—any reason why it should not equally apply to continuing offenses against the prohibitory law. The more he sought a logical answer in the affirmative, the harder it seemed to find one. He found decisions from which the inferences were irresistible. It had been held that two prosecutions could be maintained at the same term of court, one for being a common seller in January, and another for being one in February. If two, why not three hundred and sixty-five? The law always took account of fractions of months and of days, but not of fractions of days.

The next morning the court-room was packed as before, and the major part of the people stood outside because they could not get inside. If Strickland's legal position were sustained, the hearing would go on; if not, the eighteen thousand complaints would be waste paper. As representing the affirmative, he expected to open the argument.

"I won't trouble you now," said the judge. "I'll hear Brother Woods."

The remark indicated that the judge was strongly inclined to Strickland's view. Woods, ignoring the judicial decisions, made an eloquent speech on the constitutional provisions in regard to unusual punishments and excessive bail, and threatened the committee with heavy damages for malicious prosecution. Whether germane to the law or not, it was a stirring appeal to a power mightier than law—*public opinion.*

"I shall have to rule against you," said the judge.

"In that case," replied Woods, "I ask an adjournment till Monday."

"I think the request is reasonable," Strickland said.

"So do I," remarked the judge.

"Somehow," said Woods, when the defendants and their counsel met for a conference, "somehow they 've picked up an almighty pile of evidence. I got a peep at one of those books. It was written solid full of what the witnesses will swear to. They were n't summoned for bluff, and they are n't the kind we can put down as liars."

"How do you suppose they got it all?" inquired one of the junior counsel.

"They have got it, and the question now is, what to do about it. In some States we might pin the witnesses down to dates, but the rule 's so lax here that dates don't count, and Bond will stick to the law of this State like bark to a tree. It 's a dead open and shut on us, so far 's he 's concerned. It 's barely possible a jury may let us out, but I don't see how we 're going to tide it over till it gets to 'em."

"Did n't Strickland say he did n't want any of us to go to jail or pay a fine?" inquired O'Leary.

"Yes, if you 'll throw up your hands and make this an infernal prohibition town. He says if you 'll plead guilty, or nolo, to one complaint apiece for being common sellers, he 'll have sentence suspended as long as you keep out of the business, on the understanding that if you ever go into it again he 'll have you imprisoned on your plea, and prosecute you without mercy for future offenses. You could n't ask anything better, if it were n't for giving up the business. If you accept, the slate is sponged, but it 's good-by selling whisky."

"What about the nuisance act?" asked another junior counsel.

"Strickland won't stick for that. He 's found out that the old law 's a confounded sight worse than the new."

During this conversation Denman had been quietly figuring. "As I make it," he at length said, "the bail can't be less than about four millions, nor more than about eight; is that right, Woods?"

"On the whole grist? I should say it must be something like that."

"And the costs? How much will they be?"

"On all? They 'll be a fortune."

"One or two hundred thousand dollars?"

"Perhaps so; perhaps more. It 's impossible to tell."

"I would n't care how much they were, if we could hold the committee responsible for 'em. That was all bluff, what you said about malicious prosecution, was n't it, Woods?"

"Yes."

"I thought so! Now, about those costs. It seems to me we can use one or two hundred thousand a great deal better in fighting the enemy than in paying costs to the State."

"Mr. Denman, how can we fight the enemy?

They 've got all the law. They 've piled up evidence like the everlasting mountains. They 've got us solid, and you know it. There 's nothing we can do but surrender."

"Surrender!" cried the old man, with an oath. "I 'll die behind prison-bars first! I told my friends here we 'd all stand together, and lick these cranks, horse, foot, and dragoons, till there was n't a grease spot left of 'em. I 'm going to do it. They must make their peace, and let me fight it out alone. When it 's over they 'll share the victory."

"We won't do it!" shouted half a dozen.

"We 'd be glad enough to make our peace," said one, "but there won't a man of us leave you alone."

"Not one of us!" cried another. "We 'll stand with John Denman to the death!"

Every man echoed the verdict: "We 'll stand with John Denman to the death!"

"I knew it! I knew it!" Denman proudly exclaimed. "But if you stay with me, it is to the death. If it takes me to jail, it sha'n't take you there. You must leave me to save me. It is n't deserting me; it 's freeing me for the fight; and, by ——, it will be a fight before I 'm done with 'em!"

"Mr. Denman," protested Woods, "they 've got the law for every point they 've taken; and as to evidence, they 've got the representative men and women of this whole city. It 's sheer madness to stand out."

"That 's the way you lawyers talked about the rail-road. Law and evidence! I tell you I 'll lick 'em, spite of law and evidence!"

When convinced that it was not deserting their

chief, the others made their peace, as he directed. A stenographer was on hand when the hearing was resumed. Strickland filed a second complaint, the one offered before the first adjournment.

"We waive the reading," said Woods.

"Do you waive examination also?"

"No."

The first witness was a leading physician. He testified that he was called to the Apsleighshire House, took a short cut through the bar-room, saw two bartenders and all the appurtenances of a bar, also six or eight men drinking, and one paying for the drinks. He gave the names of three of the men. He fixed the date by the charge in his fee-book, which was about a month prior to the date set forth in the complaint.

Woods strenuously objected to the evidence, on the ground that it did not apply to the day in question and was too remote. He argued the point at length, and cited numerous decisions from other States.

"But the decisions in this State—" began Strickland.

"We're bound by the law of this State," interrupted the judge. "I shall have to admit the evidence."

"It's just as I told him!" muttered Woods.

When the next complaint was filed he growled, "You might as well put 'em all in together. We'll waive reading. We don't want to spend the summer here!"

The papers, filling a large basket, were filed in mass. Strickland put on witness after witness, to the number of more than two hundred. Most of them testified with extreme reluctance, but bit by bit the

truth was drawn from them.   Many greatly exceeded
expectations, knowing far more than was suspected.
Those who would have been inclined to lie, had the
cases depended on them alone, were swept along by
the great current of truth.   All were subjected to a
searching cross-examination, and Denman's stenographer took down every word they said.   The hearing lasted ten days.   At its close Denman was held on
every charge.

"In view of the extraordinary character of these
proceedings," said the judge, "I shall fix the bail as
low as the law permits.   You will have to furnish
bonds, Mr. Denman, in the sum of one hundred and
nine thousand two hundred dollars."

"It 's just as I told you, only more of it," said
Woods, when the hearing was over.   "They 've got
us solid."

"Got us solid!" exclaimed Denman.   "We know
what we 've got to meet."

If the eighteen thousand prosecutions had struck
the liquor-dealers in the full tide of business, as might
have been the case but for Harpswell's folly, and had
then been followed by complete amnesty on surrender,
the community would have regarded it as an extreme
measure.   To adopt such extreme measures against
men who had stopped violating the law was regarded
by many as an outrage that could have no justifica-
tion.   Denman was not a man to let a misunderstand-
ing of motives die for want of nursing, and the Democrats were anxious to keep it alive for purposes of
their own.   The fight was chiefly between Republicans.
The fortunes of the party in State and nation were

balanced to a feather's weight. The State looked to Apsleighshire for a majority, and as the State went so might go the Union. No wonder that thousands of Republicans stood aghast at the situation and felt bitterly toward those who had brought on dissensions at such a crisis. As Strickland had put it, he believed in the Republican party as a Christian believes in the church of Christ, and the political situation troubled him more than everything else—destroyed his appetite and drove sleep from his pillow.

The executive committee tried to stay the tide. The fact that they had to explain their reasons was against them. The ministers devoted a Sunday to the subject, thereby intensifying discord in their own congregations, while failing to reach the great non-church-going community. But the "Tocsin" reached thousands who went neither to church nor to mass-meetings. It had a stronger hold in the country towns than in Apsleigh itself. On one page it gave naked facts; on another editorials, keen, fearless, masterful, that were quoted and discussed far and wide. Every one read the "Tocsin"; it was outspoken for the enforcement of law. Every one read the "Palladium"; it was outspoken against it. The "Times" was of the hermaphrodite gender. Meanwhile the hotels remained closed, trade continued to fall off, a large industry that was expected to locate in Apsleigh went elsewhere, and people became more and more anxious and distressed.

During this period, and after the surrender of all the defendants, except Denman, on terms immeasurably more far-reaching and more easily enforced than the nuisance act, Strickland received the following letter :

SIR : The petitions under the nuisance act were made in good faith. We waive none of our rights to have the same enforced.
Yours truly,
EBEN HARPSWELL.

"I 'll put that letter among my curiosities," mused Strickland; "and as to the freak himself, I wish Barnum had him!"

VI

O'LEARY

"**M**R. CRAIGIN," said O'Leary—though of Irish parentage, he was an American by birth, and spoke without a brogue—"I 'most wish you had n't come."

"What makes you wish that?"

"I 've hated you so. I wrote them nasty, unsigned letters."

"Yes; I knew that long ago."

"You did?" O'Leary exclaimed in astonishment.

"I 'd seen your handwriting, and there were two or three expressions I 'd heard you use. It 's no sort of consequence. Don't ever think of them again."

"You knew it all the time—and have come to watch with me?"

"Just the same as you 'd do by me if I were sick and you were well."

"Do you mean that?"

"I know you would. Now, let 's not think any more about it."

Craigin smoothed the sick man's pillow, and eased his pain by changing his position. His touch was gentle, his hand cool. He had the instincts of a nurse and knew what to do. Most of all, he was full of human sympathy.

"You do for me just like John Denman," said O'Leary. "He was here all last night. He's given us flour and sugar, and tea and coffee, and meat, and all sorts of things to eat and wear, and has paid the rent for six months, and the doctor and everything; but it is n't so much that—he came himself and watched all night with me. He brought me them splendid grapes from his hothouse—brought 'em himself."

O'Leary had been caught in a machine and terribly mangled. He suffered great pain, and required a change of position every few minutes.

"I don't understand it at all!" he exclaimed, as Craigin, after patiently waiting on him for hours, was improving a quiet moment by feeding him grapes.

"What is it you don't understand?"

"How you can hate whisky as you do, and be so good to me."

"Let's not talk about that. You'd be the same to me if you had a chance."

"I want to talk about it. I shall feel better if I do. Seems as if I could n't bear the pain only when I'm talking or moving, and I'm so tired—so tired; perhaps I can lay still a bit if you'll let me talk. I want to talk about them letters and the liquor business. It is n't so much that you've come to watch with me, for you've got a kind heart and would do a good turn for a sick dog. It's different from that. You've fit the trade ever since you come to town, and you 've done more 'n anybody else to drive me out of it, and you 've known just how I 've hated you, and all about them dirty, insulting letters—and now you treat me just as if I was one of your own kind of folks and had always been your friend. You say if you was sick and I was well I 'd do the same by you. That 's what gets me."

"I have n't any doubt you would."

"Then you don't look on me as a kind of devil, to be taken care of, devil or not, because I 'm smashed up? You ain't a bit like old Deacon Follett, that sent me them tracts. Seems 's if you thought rum was hell and rumsellers human just like other folks."

"That 's exactly what I do think."

"I 've heard temperance lecturers talk as if we 'd all murder our best friends for ten cents."

"So have I. It 's an outrageous lie."

"'T would be kinder sickly for a man to talk that way about John Denman. You hate the business worse 'n they do, and treat me like a brother—as if you thought I was n't a very bad brother, either."

"I don't think so. I never did."

"But you think the business I was in was bad?"

"So bad the truth is the worst that can be said of it."

"That 's what I can't understand—how you can be death on the business the way you are, and feel as you do to me."

"Daddy," cried a shrill voice, "Daddy, Tommy want stay with 'oo!" A fine little fellow came pattering into the room. "Daddy," he repeated, "Tommy want stay with 'oo! Tommy want some 'oo eat!"

He was not clean,—this best of God's gifts to the home, rich or poor,—but Craigin took him on his knee and fed him grapes and told him fairy stories until he fell asleep.

When the boy was once more in bed O'Leary returned to the old subject. "You think my business was as bad as it could be," he said, "and you don't think I was bad. How can a business be bad and the men in it good?"

"King David was a good man, was n't he?"

"I guess so."

"He did what a man would be hung for nowadays. 'Most two thousand years ago there was a Roman emperor who hunted Christians to death and had men trained to kill each other to make sport for the people. He was one of the best men that ever lived."

"How could he be if he did such bad things?"

"No one thought of them as wrong or cruel then. Two or three hundred years ago the best of people, Protestants and Catholics alike, thought it was God's work to burn Unitarians at the stake, but they did n't think the African slave-trade was wrong. Only thirty years ago the best people in the South sold men like cattle, and millions of people in the North said it was right. Now everybody says it was wrong. It 's the same with the liquor traffic. It 's always been, just as slavery had always been. People are only beginning to find out that it 's the greatest of all curses. By and by, when they understand it a little better, they 'll crush it, and the world will move on to something else."

9

"Then you don't think a man must be bad because he does bad things?"

"No, not always. Right does n't change, but the point of view does."

"I see what you mean. I never thought of it that way before."

A few days later, as Craigin called to see his new friend, he caught a glimpse of a familiar form vanishing around a corner. On a table beside the bed were the remains of the most delicate little supper that a sick man could crave.

"Miss Denman's been here," said O'Leary, with tears of gratitude glistening in his eyes. "She sent lots of things to us the other day, and now she's come herself. See there! she cooked and brought all that with her own hands. Five minutes ago she sat by the window where you are, talking and laughing with me and cheering me up, just as if I was n't a poor man and she worth her millions; and I could n't help feeling as if she was an angel with the light of heaven shining in her eyes. Then she looked out the window, and all of a sudden I could see her face grow kind of drawn, like as if she was in pain, and first I knew she'd got on her things and was gone." O'Leary was a shrewd fellow, and he gave the editor a searching look. "She was here more 'n an hour," he continued; "and for all she's so rich and handsome, it's just as easy to talk with her as it is with common folks. I told her how you watched with me, and then —I would n't have thought I'd have darst to—I told her everything you said about the liquor business and the men in it."

"What did she say?" inquired Craigin, with a longing to know that overcame delicacy, for he and Isabel had ceased to be on speaking terms.

"She looked as she did, only not so much so, when she saw—when she went away so quick, and she said, might she give me some more chicken? That's all she said."

VII

TUNNELING

"H-TH-THE L-ord is w-w-walking in h-his g-g-garden t-t-to-d-d-day," observed a stuttering wit, as Denman crossed the common to Woods's office.

"Seen the paper this morning?" inquired Woods, as Denman crossed the threshold. The lawyer was reading one of Craigin's strongest editorials. "That young man 's got the making of a dozen Mariuses in him."

"I don't know who Marius was," growled Denman. "I know Craigin. I want to spare him if I can; but if he does n't let up after next term of court,—and he won't,—he 'll have to be put out of the way."

"Put out of the way?" gasped Woods.

"You need n't look so blank," said Denman, with a bitter laugh. "I sha'n't stick a dagger in his back. Suppose I should control a majority of the stock in his paper—the young lion goes somewhere else to roar, does n't he?"

"It strikes me, if you ever want his paper out of the way, it 's now."

"It does, does it? The thing can't be done in the middle of a campaign; 't would make too much of a howl. Besides, it may be bad for the party; but so far 's I 'm concerned, I don't care a —— about the paper till after those five hundred and forty-six complaints are disposed of. The greater the odds the sweeter the victory."

"If it is victory."

"There 's no 'if' about it. Did n't you tell the mayor and aldermen the law could n't be enforced?"

"Amounted to that."

"Tell 'em what you thought?"

"Might have colored it a shade—not much."

"Where 's your new light?"

"How could I think Strickland would take the position he has? No one ever did before, and it 's sound law. It 's the same with the evidence—impregnable as Gibraltar. Then, the cranks mean business at last, and they 've got an organ that 's a power and that can't be flattered, bought, or scared."

"Woods," said Denman, with a grim smile, "do you remember how you talked about the railroad fight, fifteen years ago?"

"Yes; and the best lawyers in this part of the country talked the same way. Because you won then where no one else could, it does n't follow that you will now. You sweat gold ten years before you came out ahead."

"The railroad folks have sweat it back three times over, have n't they?"

"Till there was n't anything more to sweat. Clifford never got it through his wool how you won. If he'd known of the buying of Smalley and the fixing of that deed, he'd have given you back his twenty-thousand-dollar retainer and washed his hands of the whole business."

"Yes; Clifford's a lawyer, and fights by the rules of the game. I won't get into a fight unless I'm right and am driven to it, and then I'll fight to win. I sold my bay mare to Tuffts yesterday."

"Well?"

"I told him I wanted to sell her because she was n't sound and never would be. He'd have paid me twice as much if I'd held my tongue."

"Yes?"

"I'd have cheated him if I'd sold her for a sound price. I sold her for just what I thought she was worth."

"Yes?"

"That was business. This is different; it's war. I can't help it. I've done everything in reason to avoid it. I'm driven to it to keep these fanatics from robbing the community of its natural rights and from robbing me of hundreds of thousands of dollars, all in the name of the law, and I shall do whatever's necessary to win. The 'Tocsin''s helping me so far's next term of court's concerned. The more it hounds on the cranks, the more it stirs up the anti-cranks. There'll be cranks and anti-cranks on every jury, and they won't agree."

"They'll let you off if they can get the least shadow of a pretext; there's no doubt about that; but how can they? The law's all against us, and the evidence is piled up like the Alps."

"Alps have been tunneled, have n't they? When are the jury-lists made up?"

"Next month."

"I thought so," replied Denman, taking a memorandum-book from his pocket. "First town 's Abbottsford; first selectman, Thaddeus Foster. You 're counsel for the town, are n't you?"

"Yes."

"Highway suit pending against it, is n't there?"

"Yes; to be tried next term."

"And you want to talk it over with Foster—before the jury-lists are made out?"

"I can't touch Foster on the jury-lists; he 's honest as sunlight."

"Money honest—could n't be bribed with a hundred thousand dollars; but who 's the rabidest Democrat in this county?"

"I should say Thaddeus Foster."

"Yes; he 's straight in everything else, and would mortgage his soul to the devil for the Democracy. He can't leave this office without talking about the effect of these prosecutions on the party, and if you suggest that all the complainants but one are Republicans, and hint that it 's a pretty sharp test for a man to stay with a party that persecutes him so, he 's fixed. He 'll turn it and twist it and chew on it till he makes himself believe I 'll be a Democrat if the Democrats help me out of this scrape. He looks on a Republican turned Democrat like a soul saved from hell; and if he thinks I 'll come in and pull hard with the elect, he 'll be mighty careful who goes on the jury from Abbottsford."

"I 'll see Foster at once. I can fix him all right on that cue."

"Next is Bunkerville—pretty much all Bunker since 't was set off. I saved him from bankruptcy in the panic of '73, and he 'd go through fire and blood for me, only he 's got a d—d stiff conscience. If he can help me and save his conscience, he 'll do it without a word being said. It won't do to say anything, any way."

Denman went on through the list. He had studied the virtues, prejudices, peculiarities, and foibles of every selectman in the county. He knew how to touch secret springs of action. He bought one man outright, he accommodated another with a loan, he gave several a tip on choice investments; but in most cases the motives appealed to were less corrupt and more subtle. One man hated ministers—the war was a ministers' war; two had grudges against Strickland —Strickland had fostered strife for personal ambition. One man had a dark secret which Denman had learned, and of which he took advantage. Another was chairman of a town library which Denman had given and which bore his name. Many had business relations with him of long standing; many were indebted for favors; many were filled with that gratitude which is "a lively sense of future favors." All knew him. Nearly all both feared and loved him. Through all the county stretched innumerable feelers, coarsely or delicately, as occasion required, but secretly and skilfully touching all kinds of motives, interests, and prejudices.

"You have n't mentioned Apsleigh," suggested

Woods, after they had spent hours in talking these men over.

"No; I don't think the city government's very fierce, do you?"

"They say it's your shadow."

"Oh, no, not that! but I guess I've a little influence with it still. Well, Woods, what do you think of the defense as far as we've got?"

"It would win fast enough if there were n't such an endless grist of evidence so strong that a man can't vote for you without owning up he's perjured."

"Do you know," said Denman, with a laugh, "that it's the weakness of good lawyers to persuade themselves that cases go according to the law and the evidence? I'm no lawyer, but I've seen a good deal of 'em. There's Clifford, one of the best in the country; same with him as 't is with you. The smartest of you stick to the theory as the old doctors did to bleeding patients to death. Forty years ago a young fellow up in Rochford girdled an orchard. He was tracked home, and confessed it to the owner and four others, two of 'em orthodox deacons. He happened to get a lawyer who believed in something besides law and evidence. He made the jury forget all about the case on trial, and they brought in a verdict that old Deacon Greene was a liar."

"Such things don't happen more 'n once in forty years," replied Woods.

"Then the time's come round just in season for me, has n't it? But that thing did n't happen. It was n't chance; it was genius. I know you won't feel hurt if I have a man with you—he can't hold a candle

to you as a lawyer—who can do anything he wants
to with a jury. He 'll give 'em plenty of excuses for
letting me out. It 's going my way. I know what
I 'm talking about, and if I did n't, I 'd give more for
one of Isabel's presentiments than for all your croak-
ings."

"There you go again on your pet superstition about
presentiments!"

"It is n't superstition. I can't account for 'em. I
don't try. All I know is, Isabel's come true."

Though Denman, like Napoleon, had his pet super-
stitions, like that great soldier he worked incessantly
and was ever alert for opportunities. For example,
just before the term of court a coarse, ill-looking fellow entered his office.

"Good morning, Mr. Bates," said the brewer, in a
most cordial tone.

"Be you alone?" inquired Bates.

"Yes," replied Denman, interrogatively and seduc-
tively.

"I—I 've been drawed as a jury," said the fellow,
coming to the point at once.

"Have you?" said Denman, after which was a long
and awkward pause.

"You 're a rich man, hain't you?" inquired Bates, at
length.

"Fairly well fixed—fairly."

"You hain't mean, nuther?"

"That 's for others to say, Mr. Bates, not me."

Another long pause, broken by the question, "Can't
nobody hear us?"

"No; this room 's ear-proof. Why?"

"'Cos I 'll tell you what, Denman,"—the low fellow felt his power and was correspondingly insolent,—"I 'll tell you what: you 're a good feller, an' I 've always liked you; gimme a couple of hundred an' I 'll hang that jury."

He had scarcely made this blunt proposal—he knew no more diplomatic way—when he met a look that astonished and paralyzed him. The cold shivers went creeping down his back, and he seemed to shrivel visibly under those keen gray eyes.

"And so," said Denman, at last, slowly and sternly, "and so you propose that we commit a State-prison crime together if I 'll give you two hundred dollars. You have given me a chance to break up the trial and send you to the penitentiary. Perhaps I shall tell, and perhaps I sha'n't; it depends—do you understand?"

"Y-yes," replied Bates, faintly, as he arose with trembling knees and slunk away.

When the door closed after him, the stern face wore a smile of triumph. "That man 's fixed," said Denman to himself. "If I 'd bribed him he 'd told of it afterward, and, ten to one, voted against me. Now he 's got nothing to tell, and terror 'll hold him tighter 'n the Bank of England."

Something was done every day. The Alps were vast and mighty, but they were beginning to be full of little tunnels.

VIII

"I MUST SPEAK NOW"

NE evening, as Denman was smoking in the library, Isabel stole up behind him, threw an arm around his neck, pressed a kiss upon his white forehead, and caressingly ran her fingers through his grizzled hair.

He drew her to his knee and kissed her.

"Papa," she said, "how goes the war?"

"Not very well, according to Woods; he thinks we're going to be licked."

"He's a good lawyer, is n't he?"

"One of the best in the State—in the regular way; but he does n't know how to shoot with an empty gun."

"So our case is an empty gun, is it?"

"Not even that. An empty gun's a good club; we have n't even a club."

"Yet you think we'll win?"

"I'm sure of it."

"You're not going to let Woods try those cases, are you? He's not the man at all."

"He'll sit in court and furnish dignity and learning. I've got a New York lawyer who can make any-

140

thing he wants to out of nothing—make a jury think the moon 's a green cheese, and set 'em smelling of the whey. It 's coming out all right."

"Yes, papa."

"Is that one of your presentiments, little girl?"

"Yes, papa. But this law business is only the beginning. The real fight is coming later on."

"I call this pretty real; and it would be hardly a growl if it were n't for Craigin."

"It is n't like what 's coming, papa. He only stands up for it in his paper now. He is n't the general yet."

"And how will it end when he is the general, my prophetess?"

"I don't know. You 'll do things to win that he would n't for worlds. You 've your millions; but, papa, God 's on his side."

"God on his side! And you too, Isabel?"

Suddenly, convulsively, she threw both arms about his neck and covered his face with kisses.

He drew her closer to him, tenderly stroked her hair, and repeated, in a voice that was full of pain, "And you too, Isabel?"

Springing from his knee, she stood before him with shining eyes. "Papa," she said, "they are trying to take your money and shut you up if you don't put yourself in their power. I have n't a word to say against anything to beat them in that. It 's right; it 's self-defense. It 's what 's coming afterward that troubles me. I told Craigin you 'd break him. Papa, how can you? He sprang under the hoofs of that great horse and saved your life! He 's so square and brave and noble, he won't hate you, whatever you do.   He is n't fighting you; it 's the miserable business."

"Isabel!"

"Papa, I 've never said anything about it before. I must speak now.   It is a miserable business, and it would be crushed out in this place forever if it were n't for you.   I was a little girl when Harry died, and I never thought much about it till within a year or two —never so much as now, till—till we broke with Craigin.   Now I can't help thinking about it all the time.   I count them up,—I can't help it,—scores and scores, rich and poor alike, that have gone to shame and death since I can remember.   They come to me in my dreams—the ghosts of these people your whisky has killed.   I saw them only last night,—dead men rising out of a sea of blood and tears,—and among them was brother Harry.   O papa! I never dared say it before, not even to myself.   Your great fortune drips with blood, papa—the blood of your own son!"

The brave, tender-hearted old man hid his face in his hands and sat like one stunned, uttering no sound.

"O papa!" pleaded Isabel, laying her hand on his shoulder, "I 'd rather take in washing than have you sell whisky.   You say the money 's all for me.   What 's a million more or less to me?   You 've twenty times as much already as I shall ever need.   It is n't the money you care for—I know that; but you 're so strong, why can't you be strong enough to give up your will?   You 'll beat them in court, papa.   I know they 've piled up the evidence mountains high, but they can't get a jury without men on it who love you, who 'd face death for you, and if that New York lawyer gives them the least little bit of an excuse they 'll let you off. Beat them in court, papa, and then shut up your brewery and open your hotels as temperance houses. If you prove that you 're mightier than the law, papa, where 's the shame of saying you 're not mightier than your love for your own little girl?"

After waiting in vain for a reply, she went on in a changed voice. There was something awful in the low, sweet, solemn tone. "I won't go back on you, papa. I love you so well, I 'll stand with you to the end, right or wrong—so well, I 'll stand with you fighting against God. Will you let your little girl do that, papa? If you hate Craigin, I 'll hate him too. If I don't hate him, I shall love him more than all the world besides—more than I love even you, papa. I can't help doing one or the other. It 's almost killing me, but, if you want me to, I 'll try to hate him for your sake."

She glided away, and a moment later Denman heard her, in her room up-stairs, sobbing as if her heart would break. "Your great fortune drips with the blood of your own son, papa!" He knew that temperance cranks had said such things behind his back, but these were the words of one who loved him so well that she promised to stand with him fighting against God—one whom he loved a thousand times more than his own life, more than everything else in the world, except his own will. The past came back to him, his joy and pride in the only pledge of his first wife's love. What a bright, brave little fellow he was! And how his life went out in horror! "I love you so well, papa, that I 'll stand with you fighting against

God. Will you let your little girl do that?" The great railroad fight, ten years in the darkest labyrinths of the law, was nothing compared with the struggle through which he passed before answering this question. Close the brewery! Open the hotels as temperance houses! Yield everything the enemy cared for! He had sworn to fight it out to the death, to die behind prison-bars rather than surrender. He had promised his friends that they should share his victory, and he had never yet gone back on his pledged word. The prohibitory law had become a burning issue instead of a dead letter. The Republican party was divided into hostile camps, and the smaller, the one with money and discipline, looked to him as its leader. The fanatics were to be scourged into abject submission, their law, odious from his point of view, was to be repealed, and a license law was to recognize what he regarded as the natural, inherent, and inalienable right of personal liberty. All this Denman had in view when he told his friends it should be no drawn battle and that they should share his victory. And at last within his heart had sprung up a consuming passion for the political honors he could once have had for the taking, not for themselves, but as the coronation of his cause. He believed in the justice of the cause exactly as he had put it to Craigin, and the desperate railroad litigation, involving his entire fortune, had developed his inborn love of victory to overmastering proportions; but he idolized Isabel. The terrible conflict in his soul raged all night. When it ended his purpose was more inexorable than ever before.

From that time he was a changed man. He gave

still more lavishly and abounded still more in acts of thoughtful kindness. If possible, his love for Isabel increased. Her conduct won his boundless admiration. She bore her anguish in silence. As the weeks went by and her form grew thinner and the roses faded from her cheeks, it was pitiful to see how he watched her and the delicate ways in which he tried to atone for the one thing he denied her. He worked and plotted day and night, and his genius shone brighter than ever before; but he aged from week to week, his old smile was gone, his old laugh had become forced and bitter. "Your great fortune drips with the blood of your own son!" "I love you so well, I 'll stand with you fighting against God. Will you let your little girl do that?" "It 's almost killing me, but, if you want me to, I 'll try to hate him for your sake!" "How can you break him? He sprang under the hoofs of that great horse and saved your life!" These words from the lips he loved best were always ringing in his ears, and, while his purpose was unchangeable, he suffered the torments of the damned. At last he hated the enemy who had stolen his daughter's heart, hated him for saving his own life, and often he muttered bitterly, "I wish the horse had killed us both!"

COLLAPSE

T was the law that Denman could not be tried until a grand jury had decided whether there was enough evidence against him to justify putting him on trial.

"Well, gentlemen," said the county attorney, on the morning of the second day that the grand jury was in session, "we 've got through with everything but the liquor cases."

"Mr. Strickland," pleaded one of the best men, "I want to be excused. I 'll tell you why. My wife died five years ago. She 'd been ailing ever since our last baby was born, and in bed all the time for the last three years. What with housekeepers' bills and doctors' bills and all, I had to mortgage my farm. Just after my wife died my barn was burned with everything in it—hay, grain, cattle, horses, farming tools, all I had. I 'd been so hard up I 'd let the insurance run out. As soon as the man who held the mortgage found out that I had n't anything to pay him with, he went right to work to foreclose. It was winter, I had four little children, and my last dollar

146

was gone. I'd always worked hard and paid my bills, and it seemed as if t' would kill me to have my little children taken away from me and put in the poorhouse, but it stared 'em right in the face. I went to the banks, and old Deacon Follett, and three or four other rich men, and they all said they'd be glad to help me if they was n't so dreadful short; they all said they were dreadful short. Then I went to John Denman and told him just what I've told you. He did n't say a word about being dreadful short. He gave my hand a grip,—seems as if I could feel it now,—and I saw two big tears standing in his eyes. Then he just sat down and wrote me a check for every dollar of that mortgage and enough to give me a little start besides, and told me I was to look out for the children first and pay him when I could. That's all I've got to say. John Denman put me on my feet and kept my four babies out of the poorhouse, and, proof or no proof, oath or no oath, I won't go against him. You may shut me up, just as you're trying to shut him up; I won't do it, all the same."

The New York lawyer who could make a jury believe the moon was a green cheese could n't have made a more effective appeal, or one more foreign to the law and the evidence. The jurors looked at each other and whispered among themselves.

"No one wants to shut you up, Mr. Adams," said Strickland. "We'll go up-stairs and tell the judge, and I guess he'll let you off."

"Let me off! I can't sit on this case, either!" cried half a dozen.

"It is n't easy to get excused; you must n't ask what

can't be done," replied Strickland, hurrying away to escape their importunities.

While he was gone the jurors talked.

"It 's just like Denman," said one. "There was Weeks. All he left was a patent right. Folks thought it was n't worth anything—said it was only one of Weeks's crazy inventions; but you bet Denman knows a good thing when he sees it! It was put up at auction to pay the debts, and he bought it for 'most nothing, and took it to New York and sold it for thirty thousand dollars spot cash. What 'd he do with the money? Put it in his own pocket, and let that sick widow and her little girl go to the poorhouse, as old Deacon Follett and lots of the pious folks would have done? Not a bit of it! He bought thirty thousand dollars' worth of good six-per-cent. bonds in Mrs. Weeks's name, and now, instead of being a pauper, she 's got eighteen hundred a year to live on. That 's the kind of a criminal John Denman is!"

"There was Willie Brown," said another, "that poor little orphan cripple; Denman sent him to a Boston hospital and paid the doctors and nurses and board and everything till he got well."

"'Inasmuch as ye have done it unto one of the least of these my brethren, ye have done it unto me'!" exclaimed a third.

"'T would take a darn sight longer to tell what he has done than what he has n't," said a fourth. "He 's the whitest man in these parts, if he is a rumseller."

"And he 's been mighty judicious in handling it," remarked another. "Has n't allowed any one to sell right and left to drunkards and boys. Held a taut rein on the whole business. No knock-downs and drag-outs. No rows. Apsleigh 's been the quietest, best-behaved city in the State for twenty years, all through John Denman."

"The temperance folks admit that!" cried half a dozen.

"It used to be a nice, sociable, friendly kind of a place to live in," said still another juryman; "and now lifelong friends won't speak to each other, and it 's nothing but hate breaking up everything, from churches to a rubber of whist. It 's just as Mr. Dow said: been the best city in the State for twenty years, and now—it 's hell."

"I 'll be hanged if I 'll vote ag'in' John Denman!" exclaimed one of the roughest of the jurors. "He 's a bird, he is, a reg'lar Jim Dandy, and if a feller wants a little suthin' in his insides, it 's nobody's business but hisn!"

"But we are sworn to find according to the law and the evidence, and if we do not we are perjured," protested the foreman.

"That 's so!" assented one or two.

"But," urged a little jeweler of bookish tastes, "it used to be the law, the greater the truth the worse the libel, and all the world honors the jury that would n't convict Captain Baillie for publishing the shameful things done in Greenwich Hospital. How was it with the Fugitive-slave Law? Who blames juries now for setting slaves free against law and evidence?"

"This is not the Fugitive-slave Law," replied the foreman. "Unless this great evil is rooted out, free government cannot exist another hundred years."

10*

"Can't it exist if Mrs. Frye has mince-pies and cider apple-sass?" piped a shrill voice. "She told my wife t' other day she could n't git no cider for mince-pies and apple-sass, 'cause her husband was 'fraid of bein' a witness."

"Mr. Foreman," inquired the little jeweler, "is it any worse for Mrs. Frye to have mince-pies and cider apple-sauce than for the prosecuting attorney to smoke an old clay pipe and drink coffee strong as lye?"

Strickland's return put an end to the discussion. The evidence was put in, piled up, as Woods said, like the everlasting mountains. Some of the jurors sat sullen and inattentive; three or four stood with their hands in their pockets, looking out of the windows; one skilfully carved his monogram on the back of a chair. When all the evidence was in Strickland instructed the jury in regard to the law, and told them that Denman's good qualities had nothing to do with the case before them. He told them that, whether the law was just or unjust, wise or foolish, was a question for the legislative, not the judicial, department of the State. He reminded them that they had taken an oath to be governed by the law and the evidence, and by that alone, and that they could not shrink from the obligation without being guilty of perjury. Then they voted. They numbered twenty, not counting Adams, excused. Three voted "Bill," four voted "No bill," thirteen declined to vote.

"Gentlemen, you must vote," said Strickland; "the law requires it. We 'll try again."

Five voted "Bill," fifteen voted "No bill."

Strickland urged them to ask questions in regard to

the law, pressed them to name a flaw in the evidence that could make a doubt possible in any sane mind, insisted that free government must be a government of law, and sharply rebuked them for violation of sworn duty. Then he made them ballot again. The ballot stood sixteen for Denman, four against him. There was no occasion for the New York lawyer who could make a jury think the moon a green cheese; the five hundred and forty-six complaints were waste paper.

The attempt to confiscate the liquors proved equally abortive. They had been stored in an isolated stone building formerly used as a jail. The commissioners appointed to examine them and report to the court found nothing but empty casks.

The November election immediately followed. Strickland, whose duty as prosecuting attorney relieved him from the odium of voluntary action, pulled through with barely a tenth of his former majorities. Every other candidate who had shown the slightest anti-liquor proclivities was snowed under. For the first time in twenty-five years city and county went Democratic on the local ticket. Apsleigh, full of dissension and hate, losing business every day, cried for peace. Prohibition was pronounced a chimera, and Denman invincible.

PART THREE

※

THE LEAGUE

I

FORMING THE LEAGUE

"SIT down a minute," said Strickland, as Craigin dropped into his office. "I want to read you this letter. It's to the chief justice:

DEAR SIR: Having decided to leave Apsleigh as soon as I can settle my affairs, I herewith tender my resignation as county attorney. The gallant fight for my last election and a desire not to shirk duty have caused me to think many times before taking this step; but, under the existing circumstances, I see no objection to being governed by my personal interests."

"That's a good letter to light your pipe with," said Craigin. "Let's look at it! I'll bet it took a day to write it!" he continued, after reading it carefully.

"What makes you think so?"

"Because it's so short, hints so much, and says so little."

"It took more 'n that, for it's three boiled down. The first was thirty pages, the second two, the third a dozen lines."

"I wish you 'd read between these dozen lines. What's the English of it?"

"The English is, we 're licked, and it 's woe to the vanquished. If I stay here I shall be nothing but an object-lesson of how men ruin themselves and their friends trying to protect the public from itself. I 've talked this over with Bradford and Harnett and several of our best men. They all see it as I do."

"You did n't talk with me."

"Good reason why! I knew you 'd say, 'Fight on!' Craigin, if going to the stake would give us victory, I 'd go there with a light heart, but it 's no use talking of 'ifs.' We 've met our Waterloo, and you 're the only man won't own it."

"There are more temperance men than liquor men in Apsleighshire, more even in Apsleigh."

"Yes, such as they are! They go to mass-meetings, sing 'Hold the Fort' loud enough to be heard a mile, put a cent in the hat, pat me on the back and say, 'Good dog, Towser! Sick 'im, Towser!' but they 're mighty careful not to get in the way of the old lion's paw."

"You 've had a mighty tough time of it, old man, and I don't wonder you feel this way, but don't you know that some of the best fighting armies in history have been made from worse material? I guess it 's better stuff than Cæsar's tenth legion was to begin with. The raw recruit turns pale at the smell of gunpowder and runs away; when discipline and battle have made him a soldier he dies at the cannon's mouth with a cheer on his lips. No matter about that now. What do you mean by 'personal interests'?"

"No one knows better than you that it 's the settled policy to divert business from every one who 's been prominent on our side. If it were mere spite they 'd get tired of it, but teaching us not to meddle with their business is the most effective way of protecting themselves. There is n't a doctor in town who can stand an organized and systematic sneering away of his professional reputation. There 's Edwards—lost all his patients on the liquor side and more 'n half on the other. It 's as bad, or worse, with a lawyer."

"Can't you make a living here?"

"Not unless you call a thousand or two a year a living. My family 's entitled to what I can earn of the good things of life. I don't want to live in a town as full of hate as this will be for years to come. I want to go where I can get on and enjoy life. It 's a bitter dose, all the same, to sell the house where my grandfather was born and where I hoped my grandchildren would be born and live and die; it 's bitter as death. But I 'm glad I did what I did, for I believe it was my duty, and we might have won if it had n't been for that fool Harpswell."

"And I tell you," replied Craigin, "we can win now. I want you to promise me not to mail that letter for a week."

He went to his office, and, writing down thirty names, studied them with anxious care. One man was wanting in tact, another timid, another rash, and so on. He drew his pen through name after name, till the list was reduced to sixteen. Then he reversed the process and with still greater care sought among the sixteen for ten, each of whom had special qualifications and all of whom could work together as one person. Though they varied widely in tastes, attainments, and social position, he believed they were the ten best men in Apsleigh for his purpose. He wrote to each, asking him to call at his office the following evening. Then he took a photograph from a private drawer, and, as he sat looking at it as upon the face of a loved one forever lost, memory went back to the dream of two years before: the yawning gulf, the shining one upon the farther brink, the armies closing in battle, Denman leading one, himself the other.

The ten came at the appointed time. Among them were those who had advised Strickland to resign. All were disheartened.

"How would it do to look at the enemy's troubles as well as our own?" inquired Craigin. "All the liquor-dealers but Denman have sentences hanging over them and can be shut up for six months at a moment's notice. Denman himself has been driven out of the business. It's a good beginning."

"A good beginning!" exclaimed one of the gentlemen. "Do you call what we've gone through only the beginning?"

"Yes. We've had the prostration of business, the reign of terror, the agony and hate; now comes the steady march to victory."

"To victory!" cried several at once.

"As surely as God reigns—if we rise to our opportunities. We've got rid of the saloon and the barroom. We must get rid of the sneak-holes and the pocket-bottle trade. Denman's influence used to be against these things; now the more drunkenness and rowdyism, the stronger his argument that prohibition can't prohibit and nothing but license can regulate. Public opinion will sustain us in this, and Denman

himself can't say a word against it. We must win
over the almighty dollar and make it fight our battles.
They say we 're ruining Apsleigh. We must answer
them with the logic of growth. If it were two thousand miles west the whole country would ring with its
attractions, and its population would double in five
years. New England enterprise and capital have over-
looked it because it 's right at home. We can boom
it with solid facts, for the public good and the triumph
of a righteous cause, instead of a money-making syn-
dicate."

"That 's something worth thinking of!" exclaimed
Harnett.

"It 's something worth doing," replied Craigin.
"You 've been all over this country; did you ever see
a prettier place?"

"No," said Harnett, "I never did."

"Places," continued Craigin, "that can't compare
with it have been made famous. It 's near centers of
business; taxes are low, and can be cut down a third.
If its advantages were known, rich men would come
here to live and to invest money. It 's one of the few
places in the United States where the benefit of long-
freight rates is n't offset by increased cost of produc-
tion incident to large cities."

"I know our position gives us long rates," remarked
Harnett, "but I 've no idea what the difference is."

"From ten to twenty per cent.," said Craigin, "and
public attention has never been called to it."

"It 's at least three per cent. a year on the capital
in my business," said Basil Hunt, a manufacturer of
fine furniture. "Hard-wood timber 's another item.
It 's the best point I know of for certain industries, and

they 're industries that employ the best class of help.
I don't see why your idea might n't be carried out on a
large scale, Mr. Craigin, if we could once get started."

"There 's where we have an advantage," replied
Craigin. "Just now there 's an epidemic of booms,
money-making schemes, most of 'em fakes. Ours will
be a novelty. Our position will be that the liquor interest, to carry its point, is trying to cripple the town,
and we, to carry ours, are giving it a prosperity it
never dreamed of. Men will talk about it. Great
newspapers and magazines will discuss it as a social
problem and write up the town as a matter of public
interest. When the city starts into new life, property
doubles in value, everybody 's making money, and it 's
understood that prohibition has brought it about,
where will the almighty dollar be?"

"On the side where it 's to be made, every time,"
said Hunt.

"Yes, and that is n't all. When border ruffians
undertook to dragoon Kansas into slavery, the best
men in the North flocked there and made homes. We
shall get the same class of people here. We must have
attractive and self-supporting clubs to take the places
of the saloons. We must educate all the time. We
must have a county organization with branches in
every town. We must have a system of quietly getting
at how every man in the county stands, and if he 's on
our side, what kind of work he 's best fitted for. We
must make our men a trained and disciplined army,
and then—then we must fight our fight."

"'Nd haow?" asked John Rogers Jones.

"The liquor interest must be smitten at the polls by

an organization more perfect than its own, officials who have been false to their oaths of office must give place to those who will be true, and the path of duty must be the path to public honors."

"We're a pretty small band to undertake such great things," remarked Dr. Bradford.

"Did n't Christ send twelve humble men to preach the gospel to the world?" inquired Craigin.

"But they had a divine mission."

"If it is n't a divine mission to lift this curse, in God's name, what is? No matter! Mohammed was a camel-driver. Buddha wandered in poverty and alone. Doctor, what 's the text about the ten righteous men who could have saved Sodom? Is Apsleigh worse than Sodom? We differ about the inspiration of the Bible, but the lesson 's the same. Ten righteous men with fearless hearts and long, cool heads can save any city, for they will be a nucleus around which thousands will rally. I 've heard of a knight who stood with a few companions and held a pass against a host until the king and his army came. He died, but he saved the nation. Gentlemen, if you 'll stand with me, life or death, we 'll hold the pass till Apsleigh is saved, till the king and his army come—the king that is the people, the army that is ballots."

"By God's help, we ten will hold the pass with you!" cried Bradford.

Not a man hung back.

"We 'll call our organization what it is," said Harnett: "the League for the Public Weal; and may its influence spread from county to county and from State to State until this great curse is lifted from the land!"

11

II

THE BILL

HE suppression of the pocket-bottle trade and the dives was a mere matter of vigilance and energy. The defendants had no standing in the community, and, as they violated the federal revenue law as well as the State prohibitory law, Uncle Sam helped hunt them down and laid his heavy hand upon them.

In the mean time a license bill was introduced before the legislature. The Democratic State convention had declared for license. According to time-honored precedent, the Republican State convention made adhesion to the prohibitory law a test of party loyalty. Many Democrats, however, believed in prohibition, many Republicans in license, and it was doubtful how far party platforms would control. Both houses of the legislature were Republican by narrow majorities. The judiciary committee was evenly divided. The sachem of the Democracy advocated license, on the ground that prohibition had never been intended as anything but political hypocrisy whereby Republicans were to have votes, cranks law, and the people whisky.

He was able and eloquent, and his voice was potent beyond the councils of his tribe. But Denman was the one man in the State without whom the passage of the bill was impossible. Others made speeches; he furnished brains and money. The anti-liquor men were also organizing as never before. On that side, as on the other, the Apsleighshire delegation to the third house had come to the front. The bill was discussed everywhere, at all hours.

"It is n't a question of morals," said one. "It 's a question of finance. The State 's full of summer hotels. There 's millions invested in 'em. Their guests spend millions every year among our people. If they 've got to submit to boarding-school rules they won't come."

"I know a first-class summer hotel," replied Harnett, "that 's always full the season through, and you can't get a glass of wine there for love or money."

"Owned and filled by some religious organization, is n't it?"

"No; and it 's one of the best-paying properties on the coast. The landlord says he won't have liquor or disreputable women about, because they drive away the best class of patrons."

"Any man who classes liquor and disreputable women together 's a fanatic. I 've no doubt there 're fanatics enough to make a few hotels for fanatics pay, but prohibition enforced would bankrupt the State all the same."

"The money, time, and life drink costs would double its valuation in ten years; would that bankrupt it?" inquired Craigin.

"If the manufacture could be stopped I'd hold up both hands for that," said a fat, red-nosed man; "but, as long as it's made, people are going to have it, law or no law. All you can do is to regulate abuses and make the business respectable."

"The other day," interposed Dr. Bradford, "a woman died in Paris. She'd made a fortune keeping a brothel. As she was dying she told her daughters she'd look down on them from her home in heaven and would bless them if they'd be good girls and carry on the business respectably, as she had done."

"I know a doctor of divinity who has wine on his table," said a flashily dressed man.

"You mean the Rev. Dr. Fielding of Seamouth?"

"Yes, sir, I do. He's a minister of liberal ideas and common sense."

"He's a good man. He has the courage to stand almost alone among the ministers of this State in opposition to what he honestly believes is fanaticism. His ears would tingle if he knew how he's talked about in the bar-rooms and worse places."

"How do you know? Do you visit such places?"

"We've collected a vast deal of evidence in Apsleigh, and one item of it is that copies of Dr. Fielding's wine bills are circulated in these places to give them the mantle of his respectability."

"I'm against rum as much as any one," urged a country member, "but if you can't stop it, why not do the next best thing?"

"Did you ever know anything to be done by saying 'if it can't be'?" inquired Craigin.

"No, I never did."

"Would you take away the poor man's beer?" cried the agent of a liquor house.

"Yes, and the rich man's champagne, and the monopoly of selling it! After the war," continued Craigin, returning to the country member, "there were thousands of political murders in the South. The feeling was so strong against the government that it could n't get evidence, to say nothing of convictions. Suppose it had tried what you call the next best thing? Suppose it had said, 'Negroes and white Republicans will be shot or lynched anyway; we might as well make this sort of thing respectable and get all the money out of it we can'?"

"It would be damnable!"

"Damnable to license crime, and right to license the chief source of crime?"

"I wish that editor would stay at home and mind his own business!" muttered a lobbyist, with an oath. "I had Hayseed fixed; now I 've lost him!"

"I don't see what niggers has to do with it!" said a cadaverous man of the kind that whisky makes thin and pale. "I denounce sumptuary laws. They 're inconsistent with personal liberty."

"That 's exactly what the Liquor-dealers' Association says, is n't it?" inquired Craigin.

"Yes; what of it?"

"And has been copied word for word into the Democratic State platform, has n't it?"

"Yes, and it 's gospel truth."

"Of course! Why don't you have a plank against burning heretics? That 's inconsistent with personal liberty, too."

"What good would it do? Nobody wants to burn heretics."

"Nobody wants sumptuary laws, either. Suppose I should call your wood-pile a heretic?"

"'T would n't make it one."

"As much as what you call a sumptuary law makes it one. My dear sir, what do you think a sumptuary law is?"

"Why, I suppose it 's a—a liquor law."

"It 's any law intended to limit private expenses. The Spartans had laws against using any money that was n't made of iron. The old Romans had a law that women should n't wear dresses of more than one color. The French had a law against wearing pointed shoes. The English had a law that only the nobility should eat more than one kind of meat at dinner, and that common people should n't eat it more than once a day. The Scotch had a law that no one under the rank of a noble should eat pie. If the United States should shut out Turkish rugs to keep people from spending their money, it would be a sumptuary law; but if they should do so to keep out the Asiatic cholera, it would n't be a sumptuary law. The liquor traffic is worse than cholera, and the time 's coming when it 'll be quarantined from one end of this country to the other."

"Not in your day, young man," cried an old farmer. "What three quarters of the people are bound to have they 'll get, law or no law!"

"If that 's so," asked Bradford, "why are all these liquor men working so hard and spending so much for license?"

"I 'll tell you why," said Denman, who had just come in. "If the legislature should make it a crime to sell breadstuffs, the flour-dealers, whether it hurt their business or helped it, would resist being classed with criminals. It 's the same with us."

So the war of words raged day after day and night after night. The Democratic leaders had promised nine tenths of their following; a fourth of it defied the party whip and voted against license. Denman made no promises; but when the roll was called, to the amazement of all, more than a fourth of the Republicans voted for the bill. It passed the House by a majority of five. But it could not become a law without passing the Senate.

The room was large and airy, the windows were open, the night was clear and cool. Why did Denman moan and toss upon his bed? Why did cold sweat stand in beaded drops upon his brow? What did he see in the darkness and solitude of his chamber?

He saw a man in the early prime of life, honored of his fellows, loved and trusted most by those who knew him best. He saw a wife whose life was in her husband, who kissed him as he came and went, whose heart had sung blithely all the day for five happy years. He saw little children clustering round their father's knee, climbing into his lap, throwing their tiny arms about his neck, hugging him tight, laughing and shouting in their joy. Again he saw the man, an outcast, pitied, despised, shunned. He saw the woman moaning out her life in speechless agony. He saw the woeful children of a drunkard. He saw the end, the horrible delirium. He heard the dying shrieks. He heard the dropping of the sods upon dishonored clay, and as they fell they seemed to spell over and over and over again a single word—"M-u-r-d-e-r." The vision changed. The ghost of his dead Harry took the place of the doomed man, and he heard the voice he loved best crying, "Papa, your fortune drips with the blood of your own son!"

Then he awoke, and though he paced the floor in agony and though his whole soul loathed the work he had to do, his purpose never faltered. It was a "necessary war measure." The position of each senator was known. They stood a tie. The license bill could not become a law unless Jared Marston was disposed of. There was no other way to dispose of him. He was fearless and incorruptible; but he had been a drunkard. He had struggled to his feet several times and had now stood five years without a fall, but the appetite was still mighty within him. If he could be made to taste wine it would end in a wild debauch, he would not be present to cast his vote, and the bill would become a law.

Denman was not present at the feast. He merely suggested his object to the nominal giver and paid the bills. The courses came and went, and the glasses stood untouched at Marston's plate.

"Come, old man," said the host at last, "this champagne is from the choicest vintage of Épernay. Just one glass before we go! Just one for friendship's sake! Gentlemen, we drink to the coming man of the Senate! Marston, you can't refuse that!"

As Marston raised his glass to return the pledge he

read the gleam of triumph in the tempter's eye, put down the wine untasted, and left the room. Next day he made the speech of the session. The license bill, not the tempted senator, was lost.

The story of the banquet, though not of Denman's share in it, got into the papers, and Isabel read it. "That was n't war," she said to herself. "It was almost murder. Papa could n't have done such a thing as that, and yet—who else would furnish that old brand of Épernay, worth its weight in gold?"

III

AN OFFER AND A PURCHASE

HE "Tocsin" was a recognized and growing power in the State; it had a constantly increasing subscription list, it was well and economically managed, and it was becoming bankrupt. Many business men declared they would have nothing to do with the organ of the cranks who were ruining the town. Others expressed regret that decrease of trade compelled them to cut down advertising expenses. The "Times" and the "Palladium," subsidized by Denman, pushed competition below cost, and the "Tocsin" had to do business at a loss or not at all. The first days of the new year were black Fridays. From the first Craigin had taken half his salary in treasury stock, which no longer had any market value. The other half was six months in arrear, with no prospect of payment. His cash assets had dwindled to six dollars and fifty cents. At this juncture he was offered an assistant editorship on a great city paper.

"Gilbert Riggs," he mused, as he read the letter for the twentieth time, "offers me five hundred dollars a month! Salary of a famous editorial writer! Queer! What can he know about me? Where have I heard of him? Ah, I remember now! He's Denman's second cousin."

If Denman, without giving up his own will, could have made Isabel happy by sacrificing ten times six thousand a year, he would have done so gladly. Craigin had no idea how much the affectionate old man's heart was set on the acceptance of this offer; but, if his suspicion of its source were correct, he knew that the gulf between him and the Denmans might still be bridged. On the one hand was a ruined paper, an unpaid salary, an empty pocket; on the other an extraordinary opportunity. There was only a bare suspicion that it might come through Denman. Why should n't he accept? Would n't he be a fool to decline? Would n't it be sacrificing a future of usefulness? Did n't ministers of Christ almost always see a higher call in a higher salary? When did a minister ever refuse to leave a weak and discordant church for a strong and harmonious one? But the salary and professional advancement, much as he longed for them, were as nothing. Love, pulling at his heartstrings, was stronger a thousandfold, and love said, "Go!" He remembered his promise of victory, the solemn compact, "By God's help, we ten will hold the pass with you till the king and his army come," his oath, "I 'll live and die doing what I believe is right, cost what it will, so help me God," and his mind was fixed. "No matter how this offer comes," he said, "I 'll stay."

"You must go," said Harnett, when he saw the

letter.   "It 's a chance of a lifetime, and we can't run much longer anyway."

"I 've declined it."

"Declined it!"

"We must hold the pass together till the king and his army come."

One morning, a fortnight after declining the offer of Gilbert Riggs, Craigin called at Harnett's house before daylight.

"It 's annual meeting this afternoon," he said, "and last night I lay awake wondering why the small stock-holders had n't dropped into the office to talk things over.   They always have before.   Not counting Abel Gay's, we 've got only ninety-nine shares we can depend on; if Denman 's got the other hundred and one—"

"It 's the end of the 'Tocsin'!" exclaimed Harnett.

"Let 's go right over to Abbottsford and see Gay," said Craigin.

Denman had had a little business with his lawyer the day before.   "Woods," he had said, "when you go over to Abbottsford this afternoon to make Gay's will, I want you to buy his three shares of stock in the Tocsin Company.   I 've picked up ninety-eight, and left his to the last because he 's so strong on the other side, but he 's such an innocent old man he won't suspect anything."

"How much shall I pay him?"

"All you can without exciting his suspicion—the more the better.   His widow 'll need more 'n she 'll have.   He 's the kind of man that 'll want to leave cash on hand for funeral expenses.   He 'll talk it all over with you, and tell you what he's got, and ask you what he'd better sell. There won't be any trouble if you work it right."

As Denman predicted, the sick man was talkative and unsuspecting.

"Wall, I vum!" exclaimed Gay, "if ye hain't an honest lawyer! I'd no idee the stock was wu'th a quarter so much. Hain't never paid nothin'. Must been layin' up money fer presses 'nd things, I guess. It's at the Apsleigh Bank. I'll give ye an order for 't now."

The offer was embarrassing, as Harnett was president of the bank.

"I won't trouble you to do that," said Woods, "because, you see, it would have to be sent down here for you to sign. If you sign one of these blank proxies it'll do for now, and you can make over the stock any time in a few days."

The proxy was signed, and Woods began counting out the money.

"I won't take a cent," said Gay, "till I give ye the stock; that's business. What's yer rush? I wish ye'd stay longer."

But the lawyer saw the doctor coming, and hurried away with the proxy in his pocket.

"Wall, naow, I do vum!" exclaimed Gay, when Harnett and Craigin had opened his eyes. "'Nd so they want to bu'st the paper? 'Nd ye say them three shares 'll do it? Gold would n't have bought 'em if I'd known it, 'nd they sha'n't have 'em naow if I can help it; but I've signed somethin'. Mother, won't ye see if there hain't some more like it?"

"Mother," who was his wife, and his junior by twenty years, produced the box of papers.

"'T was like this 'ere," said Gay.

"Why, it's only a proxy," replied Harnett. "You've a perfect right to revoke it this minute if you have n't taken pay for the stock."

"I hain't," Gay answered, "'nd, what's more, I won't, nuther!"

Woods attended the annual meeting without a doubt of the result.

"I see you represent ninety-eight shares," remarked the president of the company.

"Ninety-eight!" exclaimed Woods. "I represent a hundred and one."

"Only ninety-eight, Mr. Woods. Mr. Gay has revoked the proxy he gave you yesterday. He has sold the stock to me. Here is the certificate and here is the transfer-book."

IV

ONE TO SIX

"IT'S bankruptcy if we don't do something right off," said Craigin. "There must be people in New York and Boston who 'd give us job-work if they knew what we 're trying to do and how hard up we are."

"I had n't thought of that," replied Harnett. "I 've a friend in New York who can give us lots of printing and put us in the way of getting more. I 'll go and see him."

He got a good contract, on condition that it should be done at a specified time. With it came half a dozen journeymen printers of a class familiar throughout the country—men who journey, working but a short time in a place, the aristocracy of trampdom, bright, intelligent, reckless, turbulent. A week passed, and there were signs of trouble. The men became sullen and insolent. Their leader, known as "Stub Short," —for the reason, probably, that he was tall,—was a skilled workman, and all day his pica had looked like pi.

"We can't send out such work as that," said Craigin.

"It's better 'n we're paid for," replied Short, with an oath.   "If you don't like it, you can lump it."

Five minutes later the six new men demanded their pay and left the office.   Craigin at once wired for more help, and had no difficulty in getting it.   The new type-setters, ten girls, came on an afternoon train. That evening the editor worked late, and after he had finished writing turned off the gas and sat in one of his reveries.   The city clock struck one, reminding him that it was past his bedtime.   As he arose to put on his overcoat he heard stealthy footsteps outside. He peeped out, and in the moonlight, just under the counting-room windows, he saw the six journeymen printers.   There was a ventilator in one of the windows.   He opened it noiselessly and listened, screening himself with the curtain.

"When we've smashed his old printing-presses," Short was saying, "it'll bu'st the whole shooting-match.   They have n't got any money to buy new ones."

They were six to one, engaged in a State-prison crime.   Craigin had no fear for himself, and no compunction about killing them if necessary.   He had the build of a prize-fighter, was a skilled boxer, was quick as a cat, and had kept his muscle in good condition; above all, he was on the defensive and his presence was unknown.

A hard-wood ruler lay on his desk.   He seized it and once more peeped out.   The men were stealthily approaching the entrance of the building, Short bringing up the rear, the quarter from which danger was apprehended.   They had a skeleton key that fitted the lock. Craigin took his position close to the door, and as the first man entered he received a blow on the head and fell without a groan. The next man was disposed of in the same way. The others started back.

"There's only one man," cried Short, with an oath. "Down him!"

There was a wild rush, four to one. In taking his position at the door Craigin had the advantage of the first attack, but exposed himself to the danger of being surrounded. It was now his object to reach the double doors opening from the counting-room to his private office, for the four would then be in front of him. He retreated, getting in one good blow with his ruler. It was the work of an instant. As he reached his new position he saw a universe of stars and felt as if he were floating through immeasurable space. Some one had struck him a heavy blow from behind. He staggered, almost fell, and the ruler dropped from his hand. A foot struck it, and it went flying through the open doors into the private office, beyond the reach of the enemy. The stars, the celestial journey, passed away, and in their place the tiger that sleeps in human nature sprang forth. Craigin fought with a cool head and a quick eye. He was hit several times, for they all were at him at once, but now and again he got in a blow that sent an enemy reeling to the floor. Three and a half to one,—one man had a broken arm,—he stood them off, punishing them worse than they punished him, until Short became furious and reckless. Like Craigin, he was a quick, powerful man and a trained athlete. At some time in his vagrant career he had been a circus tumbler, and had learned how to do what would knock the life out of a man like a cannon-ball.

"Stand back!" he shouted, forgetting that the night police might hear him. "Stand back! I'll finish him!"

The next instant he was a wheel in air, then a projectile, shooting forward, feet foremost, straight for Craigin's abdomen. Craigin's alertness and agility saved his life. He sprang backward and to the left, barely escaping the tremendous blow. As Short recovered himself with the skill that had won plaudits in the circus ring Craigin's powerful shoulders shot forward and his right arm straightened like a flash of lightning. His knuckle-bones cracked and splintered as his fist met the terrible momentum. Short fell as an ox falls beneath a butcher's ax. While his comrades stood stupidly staring at him two policemen rushed in with revolvers drawn.

A few days later Craigin visited four of the journeymen printers at the hospital.

"I shall have to go to prison just the same," said Short, speaking painfully through a broken jaw; "but I have n't got anything against you, and I'm going to tell you all about it. You used us as well as anybody could. I would n't have tried anything of that sort if I had n't been hired to."

"Hired to?"

"I met a man near a lonely place I used to visit— no matter what for. It was in the night and dark, and he knew when I would be there. He told me if I'd get up a strike and smash your printing-presses he'd pay me three thousand dollars. He gave me a thou-

sand to show he meant business, and was to give me
the other two thousand that night, and hide us where
we could n't be found, and help us to get away. He
was n't far off at the time of the fight."

"Short, you 're lying to me!"

"It 's the living truth, so help me God! The man
was got up so his own mother could n't swear to him,
and he tried to disguise his voice, but I knew it just
as well as I know yours. He was John Denman."

"John Denman!" exclaimed Craigin. "Impossible!"

Then he remembered Denman's warning: "I want
to tell you fair and plain that if this thing goes on I
sha'n't shrink from necessary war measures. I 'm
outside the pale of the law, and of course you 'll
understand that, if I were to be bound by what you
might consider fair fighting, I 'd be helpless."

"I know it was Denman," repeated Short.

"Short, I want you to promise me one thing; will
you?"

"Yes, I will, Mr. Craigin. I know you won't ask
what is n't fair to me."

"Don't tell any one."

"You mean what I 've told you about Denman?"

"Yes."

"The cops found the money on me that night.
They 've been at me about it ever since, and I told 'em
the whole story to-day—everything I 've told you, and
all the particulars."

Though Short's statement was kept from the press,
it passed from lip to lip like wild-fire. The thousand
dollars found on his person strongly corroborated it,
and it was generally believed. As the community had

not adopted Denman's theory of "necessary war measures," it hurt him and his cause immensely. It helped Craigin more than almost anything else could have done. It made him the idol of hundreds who had been bitterly opposed to prohibition. It won him universal admiration. All the world loves a fighter.

Denman realized how much he had lost, how much Craigin had gained, but this was as nothing to his rebuke from the one he loved best. "Papa," she said, the day after the attack on the printing-office, "papa, you were out late last night!" He started as if a serpent had stung him, and shrank in horror from the eyes he knew were reading his heart. His daughter's face turned deathly pale, her lip curled, and her voice trembled with withering scorn as she added, "I promised to stand with John Denman, right or wrong, fighting against God; but I never promised to stand with midnight ruffians, six to one! Oh, it was *cowardly!*"

V

THE VOICE OF MAMMON

THE attempt to wreck the "Tocsin" aroused an American sense of fair play and, by bringing the Tocsin Publishing Company its share of job-work and advertising, put it on a paying basis. Craigin's pluck and popularity, his dramatic midnight victory, one to six, and the business ability and qualities of generalship he had already shown, revived the courage of the anti-liquor wing of the Republican party in Apsleighshire, made him its unquestioned leader, and won for his plans the financial backing of several wealthy men.

The city was still suffering greatly from want of a hotel. Denman had made a standing offer to lease the Apsleighshire House at a rental that would have been reasonable in ordinary times and with a thriving bar trade. Much to his surprise, the offer was accepted, and good security for the payment of rent was given. An experienced hotel man took the house, subject to conditions imposed by the League, on a small percentage of gross receipts and a large one of net profits. As soon as it was opened eleven persons under perfect system and hundreds who were fast learning system set themselves at work to make it pay. Every week a great sleigh-ride or some other entertainment ended with a supper at the Apsleighshire House. While snow still lingered on the hills a circular was prepared, setting forth the charms of Apsleigh as a summer resort and the reasons for calling attention to them. Letters were written to temperance men in all parts of the country, asking the names of people who would be likely to patronize such a house, and hundreds of women wrote to friends, urging them to take their summer outing in Apsleigh and to influence every one they could to do the same. The "Tocsin" put the case in such a way that the press from one end of the country to the other took it up and discussed it. People who had never heard of Apsleigh before became interested in it as a social problem, and it was written about from all points of view.

The problem was not how to get visitors enough, but what to do with so many. The League established a bureau. People whose houses were large and whose incomes were small were enabled to fill the one and increase the other. Apsleighshire was a river, lake, and mountain county, with fine drives and good fishing, and the bureau extended its operations to all the attractive portions of it. Taking great pains to know what kind of entertainment would be given, representing things as they were, and working for a purpose that was understood far and near, it retained and multiplied its patrons. Looking backward a few months, the filling of the Apsleighshire House seemed to belong to the day of small things. The League had made the county a popular resort and had put hundreds of thousands of dollars into the pockets of its inhabitants. As it had charged commissions, it also had a nice little sum of money on hand.

One morning the next winter Harnett entered the "Tocsin" office with a Boston daily in his hand.

"Craigin," he exclaimed, "the Crawford Cutlery Works at Steel Haven have been burned to the ground, —carelessness of a drunken workman,—and I believe we can get Crawford to rebuild here."

"What makes you think so?"

"I got acquainted with him last summer at Watch Hill. He 's one of our kind of people on the temperance question, and I told him all about what we 're trying to do. I told him about freight rates, and taxation, and cost of living, and everything. He said then that he 'd had one very costly accident caused by drunken workmen and was sick of it, and that if it was n't for his big plant he 'd come. I could see he meant what he said. We 've got the advantage of Steel Haven in every way. If he rebuilds there he 'll have to pay taxes right along. If he comes here he can get an exemption for ten years. Freight rates here are ten per cent. lower, the cost of living for workmen less, and wages about the same. Besides, Crawford 's made a large fortune and wants to live in a place that is n't altogether a factory town, where there are pleasant surroundings such as we have here, and where his family can have better society and better advantages. Let 's go down there and talk it over with him and see what we can do."

"We must take all the facts and figures we can get

that bear on the cost of doing business here," replied
Craigin. "We must be able to prove them. Seems
to me we 'd better take Basil Hunt with us, too; he 's
a practical manufacturer."

"Now that I 've got to build from the foundations,"
said Crawford, after thoroughly investigating the facts
and figures, "I 'll do it in a community that 's trying to build from the foundations too."

The money put in circulation by summer visitors
and by the great steel-works helped the League immensely. As soon as it was known why the steel-
works were coming to Apsleigh, the mighty voice of
Mammon was heard on every street corner preaching
from a new text.

VI

"R. BRADFORD," said Craigin, one Monday morning, "I heard your sermon yesterday about the seven devils."

"Yes, I saw you there. I would n't want to proselyte, even among you unbelieving Unitarians, but I 'm always delighted to see you at my church."

"Thanks! I 'm glad to go now and then. My father was of your creed almost as long as he lived, and my ancestors were, from the time of the "Mayflower." But about those seven devils! The man had one devil. He pitched him out neck and heels, and cleaned up the house, and put everything in apple-pie order. Then, pretty soon, he got so lonesome all by himself he could n't stand it, and so he went out and picked up seven other devils and brought 'em home with him and was worse off than ever. He wanted to draw the line on that kind of company, but when it came to doing it, he was n't quite equal to it. That sort of thing 's happening all the time, and we 've got to look out for it here."

"What are you driving at now?" inquired the clergyman.

"What I suggested when we formed the League. There are hundreds of men and grown-up boys in town who have places to eat and sleep, but no homes. A boarding-house is n't a home. A good many of them go into society of one kind or another and are on calling terms at private houses; more, perhaps, are members of secret fraternities, Chautauquan circles, the Y. M. C. A., and so forth; but still there are hundreds practically turned loose on the streets by the closing of the saloons and bar-rooms, with really no place to spend their evenings. We need a good substitute for the saloons."

"Such as what?"

"A place with all their attractiveness and freedom, without their evil influences—a place attractive, not to refined and educated people, but to that class of men, and especially the men that society, and the Masons, and Odd Fellows, and Knights of Pythias, and Chautauquans, and the Y. M. C. A., and the churches don't reach. It seems to me that we must have such a place, and that whether we can make a success of it depends mainly on you."

"On me! Why on me?"

"Because you 're at the head of a great church and are the leading orthodox minister in the city. No one else can put the brakes on those who will want such a place run on religious lines as you can do, if you only will. The men we need to reach won't stand it. They can go to lectures and churches and prayer-meetings and the Y. M. C. A., and all that sort of thing, if they want to, but they don't want to. If we shoot too high we sha'n't hit our game. Lots of unselfish Christian men, like Pemberton, for instance, would make it a failure; and when it comes to such persons as Deacon Follett and Mrs. Hudson—you 're about the only one in town who can keep 'em from trying to save souls."

"I see what you mean, but it sounds odd."

"Yes? If they ever saved a soul it might be different. If these men feel free to enjoy themselves, no end of good may come of it; but if Deacon Follett and Mrs. Hudson get after 'em, they 'll run like sheep."

"I 've no doubt of it."

"The deacon would n't be allowed to infest the Apsleigh Club with his prayers and tracts and to talk down to the members as if they were outcasts of God. My idea is to have what must be in the main a poor man's club with all the unwritten social rights of a rich man's club—a place where they can enjoy themselves in their own way, so long as it 's innocent."

"That brings us to the question of what is innocent, and I 'm afraid we can't agree among ourselves on that any more than we can with Denman on the liquor question."

"Perhaps so; but that 's where you can help again more than any one else. We 've got to have cards and billiards and tobacco."

"I don't see how such a club can be run without," replied Bradford, "but I don't know what Brother Pemberton will say. I 'm afraid he 'll say they 're associated with gambling- and drinking-places."

"So are oysters," observed Craigin.

"But oysters are associated with church festivals," remarked Bradford.

"Yes, in homeopathic doses. They say the rule for making church stews is one oyster to a barrel of stew. But, doctor, the devil holds his grip because so many people think what 's used for him should n't be used against him. Where 's the common sense of giving him the best of everything? Take the theater! Take "Little Lord Fauntleroy,' for instance! The play, like the story, is an evangel, teaching the simple loving-kindness which made Christ, as I think, the greatest of men, or, as you think, the Son of God."

"I don't believe even Brother Pemberton would object to 'Little Lord Fauntleroy,'" said Bradford. "Perhaps he won't to cards and billiards under the circumstances. Suppose I ring him up and get him down here?"

Somewhat to their surprise, the Rev. Francis Pemberton did not object. "On general principles," he said, "I don't approve of cards and billiards. In most cases they 're stepping-stones to things that are bad, and are almost always a waste of time; but in this case they 're stepping-stones to things that are good. Of course I 'd rather have these men Methodists and take them into my church, but I 'll do all I can to help in your way, even if it is n't quite mine."

"I 'm awfully glad you can see it as we do!" exclaimed Craigin, grasping his hand. "With you and Dr. Bradford for it, and Deacon Follett against it, there won't be the slightest trouble."

"It 'll take considerable money, won't it?" inquired Bradford.

"We 've got five thousand dollars that the bureau 's made for us. It seems to me that 's enough to start with," replied Craigin.

"Five thousand dollars!" exclaimed Pemberton. "Would you put all that into this club?"

"Why not? It is n't more than one man in comfortable circumstances would put into a house. We could n't fit up an attractive saloon with less, and we 've got to have more room than a saloon has. We 've got to have lots of room, all the appointments—plain, but comfortable—of a good club, a parlor with piano, carpets, and pictures, a gymnasium, smoking-, reading-, and billiard-rooms, a café. All these things cost money. We 've got to have a good manager at a living salary. We 've got to do the square thing if we 're to make a success of it and make it pay."

"Make it pay!" cried Bradford and Pemberton together.

"We 've made the hotel and bureau pay," replied Craigin. "We 'll make this pay. Men who 've spent dollars every week in saloons won't kick over as much every month for something better; if they do they 're not worth saving. We must n't treat them like paupers. It won't do to make them objects of charity. Suppose the dues are only a dollar a month; the billiard-tables will earn a good deal, and coffee, ice-cream, soda, mineral waters, cigars, tobacco, and the like will bring in a good deal more."

"Would you sell tobacco and cigars?" asked Pemberton.

"Yes, if smoking is allowed on the premises—and men won't come together if they can't smoke."

"But lots of people will think it is n't consistent to sell tobacco and keep others from selling beer."

"Of course! But we draw a line between tobacco and beer. If it 's right to use a thing, it must be right to sell it. If it 's wrong to sell it, it must be wrong to use it. The two things go together; you can't separate them. I don't see how a man who drinks can say a word against a man for selling without condemning himself."

The Apsleigh Brotherhood became a great success. Men who went from curiosity and because they had nowhere else to go stayed because they liked it. It was the history of the Reform Club repeated on a larger scale. Craigin won their hearts before they knew it, and those who could and those who could not understand his self-sacrifice and moral heroism loved the friendly grip of the scarred hand that had smashed the ruffian's jaw.

Meanwhile other work was going on. Through all the instrumentalities at its command the League was secretly and systematically finding out how each man in the county stood, what sort of a man he was, and, if he were with them, what he could best do. Captains were chosen, the county was divided into military districts, and secret records began to show who, in every hamlet, in every farm-house, would answer the call to arms on the day of battle that was approaching.

VII

R. CHARLES BYRD was the leading druggist in Apsleigh.

"That young man is not adapted to this latitude," he remarked one day, as Craigin was passing.

"Neither was Jesus Christ," replied a customer.

Byrd raised his eyebrows with an expression of pious horror.

"I mean what I say," continued the customer. "If Christ had n't hit the scribes and Pharisees and rulers of the synagogue he 'd have been the most fashionable preacher of the day instead of the Crucified One, the Light of the Ages. The same class that hunted him to death would drive Craigin out of town if they could!"

"Why," exclaimed Byrd, "I—I thought you were one of the old board of aldermen?"

"So I was, but I had the honor to belong to the minority that did n't vote to perjure themselves."

Ex-Alderman Capen, having made his purchase and freed his mind, went out; and Mr. Byrd inwardly

thanked God that he, Mr. Byrd, was not a sinner like
other men, and, above all, that he was not guilty of
blasphemy like Mr. Capen. Mr. Byrd was a pillar in
one of the churches. He lived on Apsleigh Avenue,
was a director in a bank, and, while not rich in the
sense that Denman was, could have put up collateral
for a hundred thousand dollars and still have had
a modest competence left. Mr. Byrd had thought it
proper to proceed against Bridget Maloney, who had
sold uncommonly poor whisky to uncommonly disreputable customers. He had approved the suppression
of the sneak-holes and the pocket-bottle trade, on high
moral grounds as well as for pecuniary reasons incident to his business. If anything further was to be
done, the prosecution of Denman was unavoidable, for
he had handled, either wholesale or retail, most of the
liquor drunk in the county. The enforcement of law
against Mr. Byrd's drug store, sumptuous with plate-
glass and mahogany, was, in Mr. Byrd's opinion, quite
a different matter.

The "drought" had caused a great demand for
"medicine." Mr. Byrd was a law-abiding druggist
with customers who, he thought, might talk too freely
or stagger into the clutches of the police. He sold to
others as "a special favor," and, as these "special
favors" were somewhat hazardous, charged accord-
ingly. The proscription of the regular trade brought
thousands of dollars to him.

One day he received an invitation to appear before
the police court, and although the occasion was not
festive nor the company select, it could not be declined.
He paid his fifty dollars and costs, and was warned

that the next time it would be imprisonment. After that he sold "medicine" more cautiously. It went by all sorts of innocent names. He did not put the store label on the bottles. He wrapped them in white paper, guiltless of printers' ink, and hid them in a dark corner of the cellar. It was months before he was again molested. The business was so profitable that his avarice got the better of his discretion and he began to conduct it on a larger scale. "They won't dare to shut me up," he said to himself. "If I 'm caught, I 'll only get a hundred dollars and costs." At last he received a second invitation, which ominously set forth the record of the preceding one and what had come of it.

"We 'll plead nolo, pay the hundred dollars and costs, and end it in the police court," said Woods, in a private interview with the county attorney.

"Can't think of it," replied Strickland.

"Surely you don't mean to insist on imprisonment?"

"That 's just what I shall insist on if he 's convicted."

So Mr. Byrd pleaded "Not guilty," and was bound over to the county court close at hand.

His case had been anxiously discussed before the second complaint was made.

"The geyser formations at the Yellowstone National Park are as delicate as they are beautiful," said Harnett. "You can destroy in a minute what it would take a hundred years to replace. Every one who enters the park is presented with a copy of the rules for their preservation, on which is conspicuously printed, 'These rules will be enforced.' The day before I got there a famous scientist threw a pebble into a geyser. The guard arrested him. 'I'm Professor Blank, sent here by the Secretary of the Interior,' said the scientist. 'My instructions would compel me to arrest you just the same if you were the President of the United States,' replied the soldier. The soldier received honorable mention. The scientist spent the night in the guard-house, was tried by court martial the next morning and heavily fined, and we met him as he was being dishonorably conducted to the boundaries of the park by mounted men in blue. A few weeks before a Methodist minister and six ladies were punished in the same way. The United States says that those formations shall be saved, and if the President went there and broke the law, he'd be punished just the same as if he were a cow-boy."

"Yet Byrd breaks the law all the time, and thinks he's too big to be punished!" exclaimed Craigin.

"He's nothing but a rich man," remarked Dr. Bradford. "He's poor compared with Denman, and he has n't any of the qualities that give Denman power."

"Does n't he count on a power Denman never had?" suggested Craigin.

"A power Denman never had?"

"Yes. Take away Denman's millions, and he'd still be a giant. Take away Byrd's hundred and fifty thousand, and he'd be nobody; but, nobody or somebody, he's a representative druggist. The prosecution of Denman hit those who bought and drank openly. The prosecution of Byrd will strike at a more influential class, those who hide under a mortar and pestle, who drink, yet want to pass as temperance men and

women. This is the power behind Byrd, the power
Denman wants against us."

"He's been fined," said Dr. Bradford, "and so have
the other druggists. It has n't stopped them. What
do you think had best be done?"

"Push prohibition to its logical results," earnestly
replied Craigin. "Enforce law in all its majesty, as
it is enforced in the Yellowstone National Park—on
the rich man's French brandy and champagne and
cordials, on the poor man's corn whisky and beer.
Denman wants us to try it, because he thinks it 'll
break us. It would have broken us a year ago, but—
the little books are getting fuller every day."

As Bradford remarked, Byrd individually was nothing but a rich man, nothing more than a druggist
buying cheap and selling dear. No one hated, loved,
or feared him. The evidence against him was over-
whelming. The jury were not of the class that hides
under mortar and pestle, and they promptly convicted
him. After the verdict, Strickland briefly stated why
he asked for imprisonment. Woods pathetically urged
his client's social position, his gray hairs, his children
and his grandchildren. The judge, remarking that he
took the prisoner's sixty years and his otherwise good
character into account, gave him two months in the
house of correction. The church of which he was a
member excommunicated him. It was a terrible example to the Apsleighshire druggists.

Byrd certainly represented the class Craigin had
mentioned, but he also represented a far larger and
more influential class, one that included on occasion
nearly all the best people in the community; and the

members of the League and others, especially the prosecuting attorney as the official representative of the law, constantly encountered expostulations more vigorous than polite.

"Mr. Strickland," exclaimed an indignant husband, "we were in trouble last night! The doctor said my wife must have stimulants at once. I had n't a drop in the house. I could n't send to Boston and wait two or three days, could I? I could n't get anything at a drug store. I tried three, and they told me they were sorry for me, but they could n't take the chances of going to jail. I could have got liquor from the city agency on a medical certificate stating the patient's name, residence, sex, age, and malady, to be a matter of public record and exposed in a public place forever, but she declared she 'd rather die for want of it than have that done. I could n't argue the case with a sick woman. I broke into a neighbor's house at three o'clock in the morning and begged him, for the love of God, to give me a little whisky. I got it all right; but I tell you, 't would be a pretty how-d'-you-do for you, Mr. Prosecuting Attorney, if I had n't, and she 'd died for want of it!"

"Mr. Strickland," said another, "I don't know the taste of any kind of liquor, but my mother is eighty-nine years old and feeble, and the doctor says good old sherry will help keep her up and prolong her life. She says she won't have her name posted with the people who are getting doctors' prescriptions for all sorts of imaginary diseases and making a farce of the whole thing, like B. Gratz Brown dangling from Horace Greeley's coat tails. I won't have my mother's

name posted that way, either. I hate to smuggle wine
from Boston as if I were a criminal, but I have to. I
used to think I lived in a free country. I 've found
out I don't, and I 'd like to move away where I could
have a mouthful of free air."

"Well, Brother Strickland," remarked Woods,
"you 're doing a good turn for the profession, anyway. Of course you know hundreds of men about
town are carrying life-insurance on their representa-
tions that they 're sound as nuts. If a time ever comes
when you 're not prosecuting somebody, you 'd better
step over to the city liquor agency and examine the
choice assortment of diseases they 've got posted up
there. When the heirs try to realize on these policies
there 'll be music for us lawyers, as sure as there 's a
God in Israel."

Craigin heard all these things and many more, and
fully appreciated them. He had come to believe that
the suppression of the liquor traffic, the voluntary or
involuntary total abstinence of the entire community,
would be the greatest public blessing that could pos-
sibly be conferred, and that it more than justified all
the annoyance, restraint, bitterness, and suffering incident to its attainment. He never forgot his oath:
"I will live and die doing what I believe is right, *cost
what it will*, so help me God!"—and "cost what it
will" included others as well as himself. While he
shrank from no personal sacrifice, he was too good a
general not to be equally ready to sacrifice others.
He was satisfied that to let the drug stores become
select and high-class liquor stores would undermine
and ruin his cause, and he saw no chance of suc-

13*

cess except in an uncompromising enforcement of law.

He had done what Denman wanted him to do. He had made the issue stern and sharp. He had included in relentless proscription—except on terms humiliating to all and intolerable to many—refined and sensitive women, women in delicate health, the aged and the sick. In the olden time the community would have risen *en masse* against it; now it was divided. The universally admitted sincerity of the man, his well-known relinquishment of the girl he loved for the cause he believed right, his popular qualities and commanding ability, the attempt to wreck the "Tocsin" by violence, the midnight fight, one to six, the making of the county a summer resort, and the coming of the great steel-works—all these things gave him a tremendous personal influence. Many people thought he had made a fatal blunder in pushing prohibition to such extremities, but no one denied that there were still two giants in Apsleighshire, each worthy of the other's steel.

VIII

PSLEIGH had a distinguished visitor. Servant-girls hastened to finish washing their dishes to get a peep at him and to hear and tell how he looked, what he wore, what he had said, what he had done, and how he progressed with his courtship. From maid to mistress, from errand boy to merchant, feminine and masculine curiosity were the same. Even the venerable Dr. Bradford forgot writing on his next Sunday sermon and sat at his study window, musing on the strange inequalities of birth and fortune long after the young man rode by. For this big, handsome fellow of five and twenty was the elder son and heir of a famous statesman, recently deceased, and in his own right was no less a personage than the Right Honorable William Percy Neville Langdon, Earl of Throckmorton, Viscount Stadwick, Baron Muer, Baron Langdon, with some of the finest estates and one of the oldest and most illustrious pedigrees in the English peerage.

Though he registered at the Apsleighshire House, he dined quite as often with the Denmans. He played tennis, rode, drove, or boated with Isabel almost daily, and she was so gracious to him that a darling hope began to revive in her father's heart.

"I don't want to dictate, little girl," he said one day, drawing her upon his knees and kissing her. "It's all in your hands. That's the American way and the right way. He's a fine fellow, if he is an earl, and he'd be a good husband to you. You'd have the world at your feet, and if you should have a son, he and those who come after him would be almost princes. I'd hate to have you so far off, but, little girl, it's— it's just about killing me to see you breaking your heart this way for my sake—trying to fight down your love for the other one." He tightened his arms around her, and, pressing her cheek to his, continued in a pleading voice: "You're my joy and pride and life, little girl. You know I'd die, oh, so gladly, to make you happy. I'd do anything in the world for you, except one. I'm an old man—a great deal older for words you have said to me, my child. I've done things that nothing but war against me would tempt me to do,—in war men are driven to things they loathe, —but I've never yet broken my pledged word. I promised my friends, who are true as steel to me,— gave them the word of John Denman,—that I'd win this fight for them, and I can't go back on that, even for my own little girl. Can't you be happy in any other way? Can't you put your father's enemy out of your heart? Can't you learn to love this fine, handsome, whole-souled young fellow, this great nobleman, who will make you one of the greatest ladies in Europe short of royalty itself?"

She twined an arm about his neck, kissed his thin

lips, and ran her fingers through his grizzled hair, as
had been her wont from childhood. Her chin quivered
and her voice was full of pain.

"O papa," she pleaded, "don't ask me! I will if I
can. I have tried—am trying; oh, you don't know
how hard I 'm trying!"

When riding with the earl next day she came suddenly upon Craigin. Their eyes met for a single
instant. In that instant she read two things, his inexorable purpose and his dumb agony of hopeless love,
and every nerve and fiber of her being thrilled with
sharp, sweet pain. "Tom said," she repeated to herself, "if he thought a course were right, he 'd follow
it straight to death, and never flinch a hair; but he 's
a thousand times braver and stronger than that, for
he loves me a thousand times better than his own life,
and he does n't flinch a hair even for love of me. I
love him! I love him! I love him! I can't help it—I
can't! I never can! And it 's killing us both."

Yet she passed him without sign of recognition, and
the next moment, challenging the earl to a race, she
put her high-blooded Kentucky stallion to his utmost
speed, sweeping up the broad avenue like a tornado,
her habit fluttering in the breeze she made, with firm
lips and flashing eyes, bearing herself like a queen
born to the saddle.

Again and again, as a proposal was trembling on
the earl's lips, she evaded it and put him off—put him
off till she could do so no longer. At last he forced a
hearing and went straight to the point, his voice quivering with passion, blunt, almost brutal, in his direct-
ness.

"Miss Denman—Isabel," he said, "you know I love you."

There was agony in her face as she looked up to his.

"You know I love you," he repeated.

"Yes, I know it," she replied in a strained voice.

"And I have loved you all these years."

"I know it," she again replied.

"It was my father's dying wish, it is my mother's, and I have your father's consent. Don't you—can't you—love me? Won't you be my wife?"

She sat in silence; it might have been minutes—it seemed eternity to both. At length she arose and stood before him. The anguish had vanished from her face in the flush of her great sacrifice. Her choice was made.

"I have had one strange, great gift from childhood," she said, "the gift of reading people as you read books. I have seen your heart from the beginning, and have known that your love for me was strong and pure and would not die. If your nature were selfish, cruel, cowardly, or base in any way, I would know it. You could not hide it from me. It is generous, brave, and loving. I know you better than you think possible. You are more than a nobleman: you are a noble man. I am a woman, and a woman's happiness, her very life, is marriage to a true man. I am but a woman, and the honors you wish to share with me appeal to me more strongly than you think. And I like you more than I ever liked any other man. But that is not love."

"O Isabel, then I may wait and hope! It will be!

it must be! it shall be! More than you ever liked any other man! That—that is all I hoped for, now."

She raised her hand imploringly. "You have not heard me through. Forgive me if I have misled you even for an instant. God knows how I have tried to love you. When you have been about to speak I have put you off; time and again I have put you off, thinking that perhaps I might. If I have let you hope in vain, forgive me for the pain I have caused you, for I have longed to love you. It would have been, it would be now, more than life; it would be release from agony."

"Release from agony? O Isabel!"

"Yes, release from agony. If I marry you, I must pledge my word to love you. My father is a plain, self-made man, a brewer, but no word of belted knight was ever held more sacred than his. John Denman's daughter cannot take your love, your name, your title, and give you empty vows."

"But, Isabel, I won't ask you to love me as I love you—not yet. I 'll wait and hope."

"I have not yet told you all. I love another man. I have tried to think I hated him; I have tried to hate him, but love is stronger than my will. The more I have tried to hate him, the more I have loved him. I love him with my whole heart and soul, with all my life, and he loves me, though he has never told me so in words; and I can never marry him, never speak to him. He is my father's enemy."

With lifted head and shining eyes she stood before him. Then suddenly she turned, and, dropping on a sofa, sobbed as if her heart were broken.

IX

THE CONVENTION

ONCE in six years congressional conventions were held in Apsleigh. It was Apsleigh's turn. The occasion always brought many people into town, and the intensity of the struggle between Denman and Strickland would naturally bring a far greater number than usual; but the shrewdest politicians in Denman's camp were amazed at what they saw. The incoming trains were packed. At stations for twenty miles around crowds were waiting for means of transit. Extra trains were put on. Every railway line, every highway, was thronged, and all roads led to Apsleigh. The little city overflowed with men. When asked the cause, thousands gave the same reply: "We're sent for."

The delegates were divided into three classes, about equally numerous: those pledged to Denman, those pledged to Strickland, those unpledged and doubtful. Woods presented Denman's name. He made a strong speech, but it lacked the ring of confidence. Every Denman delegate knew that the incoming of thousands from the country was a bad omen.

When Woods sat down, Strickland took the floor

with a large package of little books under his arm. A murmur ran through the hall. Was he going to the indecent length of presenting his own name? Or was it some new surprise? He began by saying that he had allowed his own name to be used simply to aid in a conspiracy to nominate Craigin without his knowledge and in spite of his refusal to be a candidate. The wild and prolonged applause that greeted this announcement showed what a master stroke of policy it was and carried consternation to Denman's followers. Then Strickland sketched the man's career during the four years he had lived in Apsleigh. It was slow work, for every few sentences his voice was drowned with cheers, and, as he dramatically touched upon the saving of Denman's life and the midnight fight, one to six, the cheers swelled into a deafening roar. When it subsided he plied his hearers with prosaic facts and figures: the rise in real estate shown by recent sales, the increase in savings-bank deposits and in taxable property, the decrease in the rate of taxation, in the amount of unpaid taxes, of worthless store accounts and chattel mortgages.

"Our State conventions," he continued, "have long made adhesion to the prohibitory law a test of party loyalty. Mr. Denman has accumulated millions by violating that law. He bolted the nomination of a Republican candidate for mayor and defeated him, bolted my nomination and almost defeated me, solely in the liquor interest. He has made it impossible to elect city governments and city marshals that would be true to their oaths of office. Time and again he has refused the highest political honors this State could give him; now he prostitutes his genius and spends money without stint, as it never before was spent in this State, simply and solely to force the coronation of a traffic that for nearly forty years has been legislated against as a crime. The issue is squarely raised in this district, and must be met."

As the music of a distant band floated through the open windows his manner changed and became almost majestic. "I had almost forgotten," he said, "that I am not here to plead for Craigin's nomination. I am here to demand it as the representative of irresistible power. Six hundred and thirty-two of the temperance Democrats of Apsleighshire are pledged to vote for me; every man of them and hundreds more will vote for Craigin. Where are the two hundred and ninety-one third-party voters of this county? All but Harpswell and some twenty more are back in the ranks of temperance Republicans. What are these little books? They are the result of eighteen months of secret, patient, systematic work. They are the muster-roll of an army. They contain the names of three thousand five hundred and fifty-eight Republicans of Apsleighshire who are pledged to vote for me; and because Denman has bolted candidates for loyalty to our party platforms, every man of them is pledged to scratch or paste his name. This is what they would do for me; but for Craigin—it will be personal devotion to a beloved chief."

From the distant Miller Block came the roar of thousands of voices cheering themselves hoarse. "Do you hear that?" he continued. "The Strickland banners are called in. The Craigin banners are unfurled. The work that has been done secretly in this county will be done openly in other counties. Picked men will visit every village, every farm-house, telling the story of the great fight for the enforcement of the law, pledging votes for the man who has brought victory out of defeat and has recreated Apsleighshire. If the impossible should happen, if Denman should be nominated, the same work will be done against him."

The wild cheers, drawing nearer and nearer, drowned the speaker's voice. At last, watching an opportunity to make himself heard, he shouted, "The knight has held the pass! Look out the windows! The king and his army have come!"

The delegates rushed to the windows. Down the street, far as the eye could reach, was a line of men. A band was at the head of the column, playing "Hail to the Chief!" Next came the clergy of Apsleighshire, bearing the motto, "God and our homes. Every vote for Craigin. Not a vote for Denman." Then five hundred business men of Apsleigh, on their banner, "Prohibition has filled our pockets. Every vote for Craigin. Not a vote for Denman." Then Crawford, at the head of two hundred and fifty of his workmen, their motto, "Prohibition brought us to Apsleigh. Every vote for Craigin. Not a vote for Denman." Then smaller industries, with their mottos. Then the Apsleigh Brotherhood, four hundred strong, with a beautiful silken flag, on which was embroidered a bloody right hand, and below it the words in great letters of pure gold, "Licked them, one to six. Every vote for Craigin. Not a vote for Denman." Of all the banners, no other was cheered like this—cheered till it seemed as if the little city rocked with the sound; for nothing else had made Craigin so many friends, and cost Denman so many, as that grim midnight fight. Last of all came the farmers from every hill and valley of Apsleighshire, town by town, in long array. Their mottos showed how Mammon had won them. There they were, near two thousand strong, every vote for Craigin, not a vote for Denman. The secrecy and long repression were over. The substitution of their beloved leader's name set his followers wild with enthusiasm. The clamor of the band was unheard amid the singing and the shouting of that long array of men. The king and his army had come. There was no enemy that could stand before them.

"Woods," exclaimed one of the Denman leaders, when at length a semblance of order was restored in the convention, "Woods, you must withdraw our candidate."

"No, I won't," snarled Woods. "I 'd rather face wolves than face John Denman if I did."

"But you must. You can't stand out in the face of all this."

"What does he care for this compared to hauling down his colors?"

"Then let him sink alone! He can't take the party with him. Mr. Chairman," cried the delegate, standing on a chair and shouting at the top of his voice, "Mr. Chairman, as one of the original Denman men, I move that William Henry Craigin be nominated by acclamation."

The motion carried. Five minutes later cannon thundered from a neighboring hill and church bells rang forth their merriest peals.

X

"O DEATH, WHERE IS THY VICTORY?"

ENMAN sat in the home office which he called his library. In all but years he had grown very old. Though he had aged rapidly for months, he was older by a decade than when he had left the house that morning. He had come home at noon, confused, apathetic. Isabel sat on a low stool beside him, with her head on his knee and holding his hand, as she had used to do when she was a little child. She did not speak, but often kissed his long, thin fingers and looked up into his face.

At length, although the Denman mansion was distant from the business portion of the town, the music of a band and the shouting of men became distinctly audible. Then came the ringing of bells and the booming of cannon. Denman seemed not to hear. He sat in a stupor, with his head on his hand. A sharp ring at the telephone aroused him. In going to the instrument, only a few steps away, he staggered like a drunken man.

"The worst has happened," said the voice. "Craigin has been nominated by acclamation."

There was a heavy fall. Denman was stricken with apoplexy.

After several hours consciousness returned. His right side was paralyzed; his face was drawn; his left eye remained open and immovable. His mind was clear. He could talk but little and with great difficulty.

"Doctor," he said, "tell me the truth: shall I live or die?"

"I think it's possible you may live for months."

"As I am?"

"I'm afraid so."

"So bad as that?" he said. "I hoped it would be death."

"It may be, Mr. Denman. You will have another shock. It may not come for weeks or months. It may come any time."

"May come any time?"

Death, even the living death of a paralytic, was nothing to Denman compared with the bitterness of defeat. He longed to die, for his pledge was unfulfilled and his power to keep it was broken; but he had one ruling passion left to gratify—his love for Isabel.

A distinguished specialist, summoned by telegraph, was ushered in.

"Doctor," said Denman, "for God's sake, tell me the truth: how soon is the next stroke coming?"

As the great specialist looked at the sick man he saw at a glance what the other had failed to note, and promptly answered, "It's on you now. If you have anything to say, say it instantly. Your time is measured by seconds."

A flash of the old unconquerable will lighted the

stricken man's face. "Tell Dick," he said, "he shall have ten thousand dollars if he gets Craigin here while I can speak."

Seconds passed, and a carriage and pair standing at the door tore down the long avenue with the speed of the wind. Seconds lengthened into minutes. In the halls and other rooms of the great house faithful servants grieved for a master who had been always generous, always kind. In a corner of her husband's bedroom Mrs. Denman hysterically sobbed and shrieked unheeded. Isabel knelt beside her father, uttering no sound, pressing his unparalyzed hand to her lips, gazing into his face with great, dry, anguish-stricken eyes. The two physicians—there was naught else they could do—stood at the bedside and saw a strange, an awful, an heroic thing.

Convulsively gripping his daughter's hand, the dying man set his teeth and fixed his unparalyzed eye on the great clock by the wall. Tick, tick, tick—slowly and solemnly the second-hand went round; tick, tick, tick, and the long minute-hand moved—moved as if it were measuring the ages of eternity. Tick, tick, tick—sixty seconds like hours, and again it moved. Once, twice, thrice, five, ten, fifteen, twenty—twenty times it moved. Twenty awful minutes, and still the teeth were set, the eye was fixed and undimmed, and the grim fight for another inch of life went on. "It's almost a miracle," whispered the specialist to his medical brother. "The stroke was falling as I entered. The man is holding death back by the sheer power of his will."

Cragin had been kept from the convention on the

pretext that his presence would make it more difficult
to prevent a stampede from Strickland to himself.
His name mingled with cheers and borne on banners
was his first intimation of the conspiracy to nominate
him. The procession marched by, singing and shouting. It came back and gathered in a dense mass before his office. Strickland, Harnett, and others rushed
in. "You 're nominated," they exclaimed, "and must
make a speech!"

He was dazed, and knew not what to say. They led
him to a little balcony in front of his office windows.
He was greeted with a mighty shout. Then all was
still. He stood speechless, vainly trying to collect
himself. Some one entered the balcony and said,
"John Denman is dying." The crowd below, wondering at the delay, broke forth in renewed cheers.
Craigin tried to tell them, and his voice failed him.

"Fellow-citizens," said Harnett, coming to the rescue,
"we have just received sad news. It is reported that
Mr. Denman is dying."

There was no more thought of speeches; there were
no more cheers. All at once, as never before,—not
even in the days of his unquestioned power,—men
realized Denman's greatness of soul, his fidelity to his
friends, his dauntless courage, his ever-abounding gen-
erosity, his acts of thoughtful kindness, his cheerful
words, his genial smile, the cordial, honest grasp of his
hand. Of the thousands who had banded together to
break his power, hundreds had shared his bounty and
all had felt its influence. The very churches whose
bells had joyously pealed over his defeat had received
largely of his gifts. In all ways, save one, he had been

so great a public benefactor, so wise and strong and good, overshadowing all about him less by his millions than by his greatness and his graciousness, it seemed as if he could not die. Men spoke through tears, almost in whispers. An awful silence reigned in Apsleigh.

Craigin found himself seated in his office chair, scarcely knowing how he got there. Friends were around him, but when they spoke to him he answered in monosyllables and absently. They understood and silently withdrew. The past came up before him. Again he seemed to feel Tom Andrews's arms around his neck and hear him saying: "The more chance there is of struggle and sacrifice for an ideal, the more you 'll persuade yourself it 's your duty." "We 've been like brothers for seven years, chum, and I love you better than any one else in the world except my mother, and next to you I love Uncle John. As sure as you go, chum, there 'll misery come of it." "I know it is n't a bit of use, but I can't help saying, don't go !" Again he seemed to hear Denman say: "There are horses and dogs and guns and boats and fishing-tackle at your service. There 's always a spare knife and fork at our table; drop in as often as you can—breakfast, lunch, or dinner. We all play whist. We want you to come and go just as Tom would if he were living here." Again he seemed to go and come, less as a welcome guest than as a member of the family. The agonizing struggles in his own soul came back to him—love pulling at his heartstrings, the blind groping in anguish of spirit to know what duty was, and the solemn oath, "I 'll live and die doing what I *believe* is right, cost what it will, so help me God!"

15

He had kept his oath; he had done what he *believed* was right; but was it right?

In his first awful struggle with himself he thought he heard a still, small voice saying, "Yes." In his agony and doubt and darkness he took it for the voice of God. "The more chance there is of struggle and sacrifice for an ideal," said Tom, "the more you'll persuade yourself it's your duty." Had he persuaded himself? Was that still, small voice from heaven the imagination of a racked and tortured soul? Now he seemed to hear the same voice, stern and relentless, in thunder tones demanding, "Was it right?"

He saw Apsleigh as it was when first he came—easy-going, gay, social, full of kindliness. Again he saw Apsleigh and Apsleighshire, divided into trained, disciplined, and hostile camps, full of hate, every man's hand against his neighbor, every man watching his neighbor's acts and writing down his neighbor's words; total abstinence from intoxicating drink (the one supreme private virtue) and compelling all others to abstain (the supreme public virtue), twin-sister virtues, linked hand in hand. And then he heard, as it seemed to him, a voice from the dead, saying: "Higher than any finite court or law or constitution is the primary, eternal, and inalienable right of man to eat and drink in moderation, with decent regard for the rights and feelings of others. A prohibitory law is such an outrageous and intolerable meddling with personal liberty that anything necessary to resist it is justifiable; and I want to tell you fair and plain that if this thing goes on, I sha'n't shrink from necessary war measures."

The burden and intense strain of the long contest

would have broken a weaker man, and, exhausted as
he was, the terrible shock had unnerved him. He
could not reason; he could only feel. Many hours
wore away, night came, and still he sat alone in his
misery, his elbows on his knees, his face buried in his
hands, the voice thundering in his ears, "Was it right?"
Visions of horror came to him. Again he saw the
yawning gulf, the armies closing in battle, the shining
one upon the farther side. All tenderness and re-
proach had gone from her eyes. They gleamed on
him from an infinite distance, hard and cold and piti-
less, like stars on a midwinter night. The vision
changed. He saw a spacious chamber, a grandfather's
clock by the wall, a great, four-posted bed, a dead man
lying on it, a beautiful girl kneeling beside him, her
arms around him, kissing his cold lips, bathing his
white face with her tears, sobbing her life away. He
had no thought, no hope for himself, but his whole
heart went out to her in her agony of grief, and as he
tried to speak she sprang to her feet and shrieked,
"You killed him! You killed him!" As he shrank
back, appalled and conscience-stricken, beside her rose
a terrible, great mountain, clothed round about with
smoke and flame and lightnings, and from their midst
he heard an awful voice, like the voice of God from
Sinai, inexorably demanding, "Was it right?"

The sound of horses coming down the street at
breakneck speed aroused him. A carriage dashed up
to the door. A coatless, hatless man rushed in, stum-
bling in the darkness.

"Quick!" he exclaimed, "quick! John Denman's
dying! He wants yer!"

Instantly Craigin was in the carriage and was whirled away. The moment it stopped he was out and up the steps, three at a bound.

"Craigin," said Denman, at once, "we've both done wrong. I want to be your friend—more than your friend. Isabel, Craigin, I shall die happy—happy if you promise me that nothing of all this shall stand between you two."

Dropping on his knees beside the dying man, Craigin clasped his hand and Isabel's, and said, "I promise."

"I promise too," said Isabel.

The poor drawn face lighted up with the old loving smile, a smile so full of love and joy and peace, it seemed as if heaven were shining there.

"Isabel, little gir—"

While the pet name was on his lips the angel of death smote him, and his brave spirit passed from earth.

APPENDIX

APPENDIX

"Blessed are the peacemakers: for they shall be called the children of God."—Jesus, Matt. v. 9.

"Think not that I am come to send peace on earth: I came not to send peace, but a sword. For I am come to set a man at variance against his father, and the daughter against her mother, and the daughter-in-law against her mother-in-law. And a man's foes shall be they of his own household."—Jesus, Matt. x. 34–36.

"Be not among winebibbers; among riotous eaters of flesh: for the drunkard and the glutton shall come to poverty: and drowsiness shall clothe a man with rags."—Solomon, Prov. xxiii. 20, 21.

"The Son of man came eating and drinking, and they say, Behold a man gluttonous, and a winebibber, a friend of publicans and sinners. But wisdom is justified of her children."—Jesus, Matt. xi. 19.

"Who hath woe? who hath sorrow? who hath contentions? who hath babbling? who hath wounds without cause? who hath redness of eyes? They that tarry long at the wine; they that go to seek mixed wine. Look not thou upon the wine when it is red, when it giveth his color in the cup, when it moveth itself aright. At the last it biteth like a serpent, and stingeth like an adder."—Solomon, Prov. xxiii. 29–32.

"And the third day there was a marriage in Cana of Galilee; and the mother of Jesus was there: and both Jesus was called, and his disciples, to the marriage. And when they wanted wine, the mother of Jesus saith unto him, They have no wine. Jesus saith unto her, Woman, what have I to do with thee? mine hour is not yet come. His mother saith unto the servants, Whatsoever he saith unto you, do it. And there were set there six water-pots of stone, after the manner of the purifying of the Jews, containing two or three firkins apiece. Jesus saith unto them, Fill the water-pots with water. And they filled them up to the brim. And he saith unto them, Draw out now, and bear unto the governor of the feast. And they bare it. When the ruler of the feast had tasted the water that was made wine, and knew not whence it was, (but the servants which drew the water knew,) the governor of the feast called the bridegroom, and saith unto him, Every man at the beginning doth set forth good wine ; and when men have well drunk, then that which is worse : but thou hast kept the good wine until now. This beginning of miracles did Jesus in Cana of Galilee, and manifested forth his glory ; and his disciples believed on him."—John ii. 1-11.

"Wine is a mocker, strong drink is raging : and whosoever is deceived thereby is not wise."—Solomon, Prov. xx. 1.

"Drink no longer water, but use a little wine for thy stomach's sake and thine often infirmities."—St. Paul, 1 Tim. v. 23.

"Woe unto him that giveth his neighbor drink, that puttest thy bottle to him, and makest him drunken also, that thou mayest look on their nakedness !"—Hab. ii. 15.

"He watereth the hills from his chambers : the earth is satisfied with the fruit of thy works. He causeth the grass to grow for the cattle, and herb for the service of man : that he may bring forth food out of the earth ; and wine that maketh glad the heart of man, and oil to make his face to shine, and bread which strengtheneth man's heart."—David, Ps. civ. 13-15.

"Now if it be true that a vast proportion of the crimes which government is instituted to prevent and repress have their origin in the use of ardent spirits ; if our poorhouses, workhouses, jails, and penitentiaries are tenanted in a great degree by those whose first and chief impulse to crime came from the distillery and the dram-shop ; if murder and theft, the most fearful outrages on property and life, are most frequently the issues and consummation of intemperance,—is not government bound to restrain by legislation the vending of the stimulus to these terrible social wrongs? Is government never to act as a parent, never to remove the causes or occasions of wrong-doing? Has it but one instrument for repressing crime, namely, public, infamous punishment, an evil only inferior to crime? Is government a usurper? Does it wander beyond its sphere by imposing restraints on an article which does no imaginable good; which can plead no benefit conferred on body or mind; which unfits the citizen for the discharge of his duty to his country; and which, above all, stirs up men to the perpetration of most of the crimes from which it is the highest and most solemn office of government to protect society?"—Channing, Works, vol. ii., p. 377.

"The object of this essay is to assert one very simple principle, as entitled to govern absolutely the dealings of society with the individual in the way of compulsion and control, whether the means used be physical force in the form of legal penalties, or the moral coercion of public opinion. That principle is that the sole end for which mankind are warranted, individually or collectively, in interfering with the liberty of action of any of their number, is self-protection; that the only purpose for which power can be rightfully exercised over a member of a civilized community, against his will, is to prevent harm to others. His own good, either physical or moral, is not sufficient warrant. He cannot rightfully be compelled to do or forbear because it will be better for him to do so, because it will make him happier, because, in the opinions of others, to do so would be wise or even right. . . . Without dwelling upon supposititious cases, there are in our own day gross usurpations upon the liberty of private life actually practised, and still greater ones threatened, with some expectation of success, and opinions proposed which assert an unlimited right in the public not only to prohibit by law everything which it thinks wrong, but, in order to get at what it thinks wrong, to prohibit any number of things which it admits to be innocent. Under the name of preventing intemperance, the people of one English colony and of nearly half the United States have been interdicted by law from making any use whatever of fermented drinks, except for medical purposes; for prohibition of their sale is in fact, as it is intended to be, prohibition of their use. And though the impracticability of executing the law has caused its repeal in several of the States which had adopted it, . . . an attempt has been commenced, and is prosecuted with considerable zeal by many of the professed philanthropists, to agitate for a similar law in this country. The association, or 'Alliance,' as it terms itself, which has been formed for this purpose, has acquired some notoriety through the publicity given to a correspondence between its secretary and one of the very few English public men who hold that a politician's opinions ought to be founded on principles. . . . The [secretary] of the Alliance, . . . however, says: 'I claim as a citizen a right to legislate whenever my social rights are invaded by the social act of another.' And now for the definition of these 'social rights.' 'If anything invades my social rights, certainly the traffic in strong drink does. It destroys my primary right of security by constantly creating and stimulating social disorder. It invades my right of equality by deriving a profit from the creation of a misery I am taxed to support. It impedes my right to free moral and intellectual development by surrounding my path with dangers, and by weakening and demoralizing society, from which I have a right to claim mutual aid and intercourse.' A theory of 'social rights' the like of which probably never before found its way into distinct language, being nothing short of this: that it is the absolute social right of every individual that every other individual shall act in every respect exactly as he ought; that whosoever fails thereof in the smallest particular violates my social right and entitles me to demand from the legislature the removal of the grievance. So monstrous a principle is far more dangerous than any single interference with liberty; there is no violation of liberty which it would not justify; it acknowledges no right to any freedom whatever, except perhaps to that of holding opinions in secret without ever disclosing them; for the moment an opinion which I consider noxious passes any one's lips it invades all the 'social rights' attributed to me by the Alliance. The doctrine ascribes to all mankind a vested inter-

est in each other's moral, intellectual, and even physical per-
fection, to be defined by each claimant according to his own
standard."—John Stuart Mill, "Essay on Liberty."

"Virtue must come from within; to this problem religion and
morality must direct themselves. But vice may come from without; to hinder this is the care of the statesman."—Professor
F. W. Newman.

"It is mere mockery to ask us to put down drunkenness by
moral and religious means."—Cardinal Manning.

"The principle of prohibition seems to me to be the only safe
and certain remedy for the evils of intemperance. This opinion
has been strengthened and confirmed by the hard labor of more
than twenty years in the temperance cause."—Father Mathew.

"Liberty is a means and not an end."—Dr. Arnold.

"Wholesome laws preserve us free
By stinting of our liberty."

"No man oppresses thee; . . . but does not this stupid pew-
ter pot oppress thee?"—Thomas Carlyle.

"Between the one extreme of entire non-interference, and the
other extreme in which every citizen is to be transformed into a
grown-up baby with bib and pap-spoon, there lie innumerable
stopping-places; and he who would have the state do more than
protect is required to say where he means to draw the line, and
to give us substantial reasons why it must be just there and
nowhere else."—Herbert Spencer, "Social Statics," p. 316.

"The [Maine] law of itself, under a vigorous enforcement of
its provisions, has created a temperance sentiment which is mar-
velous and to which opposition is powerless. In my opinion,
our remarkable temperance reform of to-day is the legitimate
child of the law."—Senator William P. Frye.

"I have the honor unhesitatingly to concur."—Senator Lot
M. Morrill.

"I concur in the foregoing statements; and on the point of the relative amount of liquors sold at present in Maine and in those States where a system of license prevails, I am very sure, from personal knowledge and observation, that the sales are immeasurably less in Maine."—James G. Blaine.

"Men who have not the strength of mind to act thus [to control their appetites] will not be made more self-reliant or more fit to wrestle with the many temptations of the world by being put into leading-strings and kept out of the sight of beer."—Wordsworth Donisthorpe, "Individualism: A System of Politics," p. 79.

"There it stands, a shield to all the youth of the county against the temptation to form drinking habits. Under its benign influence the number of tipplers is steadily decreasing, and fewer young men begin to drink than when licensed houses gave respectability to the habit. . . . It is as readily enforced as are the laws against gambling, licentiousness, and others of similar character. Its effect as regards crime is marked and conspicuous. Our jail is without inmates, except the sheriff, for more than half the time."—John S. Mann.

"The dangers in the road of social reconstruction under government control are so grave that they can scarcely be exaggerated, dangers arising not only from the serious chance of inefficiency in the methods chosen, but from the transfer of responsibilities by the establishment of national law in the place of individual duty; from the withdrawal of confidence in the qualities of men in order to bestow it on the merits of administrations; from the growing tendency to invoke the aid of the state, and the declining belief in individual power."—G. J. Goschen.

"The effect of prohibitory laws is strikingly shown by the comparatively vacant apartments in the jails of counties where the local-option law is in force."—Commissioners of Public Charities of the State of Pennsylvania.

"I fail to see that decentralization can be an antidote to democratic despotism. . . . Local despotism is the worst despotism. Decentralization cannot go further than the family, and what kind of local government is more loathsome than the unchecked rule of a brutal paterfamilias? Local option in regard to liquor and to other matters is part and parcel of a system of decentralization which, for the trampling under foot of private liberty and the crushing out of individuality, has no equal among modern forms of government."—Donisthorpe, "Individualism," p. 88.

"What has become of this mass of corruption and disgusting vice? . . . The Maine Law has swept it away forever."—Davis, "Maine Law Vindicated."

"The good old saying that you cannot make people moral by act of Parliament has been and still is disregarded, but not with impunity. Surely the state, which has conspicuously failed in every single department of moralization by force, may be wisely asked in future to mind its own business."—Donisthorpe, "Essay on the Limits of Liberty."

"A law, even when public sentiment is not exactly ready for it, if its intention is supported by the public conscience, if its operation naturally leads to better order, to greater happiness and lower taxation, has a certain victory. Unquestionably the Maine Law had it."—George William Curtis.

"The ultimate issue of the struggle is certain. If any one doubts the general preponderance of good over evil in human nature, he has only to study the history of moral crusades. The enthusiastic energy and self-devotion with which a great moral cause inspires its soldiers always have prevailed, and always will prevail, over any amount of self-interest or material power arrayed on the other side."—Goldwin Smith.

"The scale on which intoxicating drinks are used is enormous; the revenues derived by governments from this source are of the greatest importance; the persons concerned in vending them as their entire business, or a part of it, are more numerous in cities than those who pursue any other trade; many employments could not succeed without adding this sale to their other business; and the most contrary opinions have currency in respect to dealing with this vast evil of the United States and of other

Northern nations. There is no dispute as to the magnitude of the evil; the dispute touches the right, the feasibility of repressing it, and the best way of so doing. . . . Prohibition has been supported on other grounds besides that of the evil growing out of the sale and use of strong drink. It has been classed with the sale of poisons, because the alcohol unmixed is a noxious substance in the system. It has been said that to touch anything which can intoxicate is a sin on account of the example thus placed before the weak, which, if it were true, would only affect the action of individuals acting in the light of personal duty, but could not be a ground for legislation. It has been claimed that much of the inferior spirituous liquor is adulterated, which may be true, as it is of coffee, sugar, and even flour. But this, while it calls for police inspection of the articles sold in the shops, does not of itself call for prohibition. The grocer is bound to ascertain, as far as he can, that his articles are what they pretend to be and contain no noxious ingredients. And this will be generally known by the price which is charged to him and by the reputation which certain sellers or manufacturers acquire. And there are chemical and other tests of spirituous liquors. Prohibition, then, if the best means for suppressing drunkenness, must be looked at simply as a means of getting rid of a very enormous evil in society. Is it, or is it likely to become, an effectual preventive? Experience in this country has proved that it is not effectual."—Woolsey, "Political Science," vol. ii., p. 426.

"Law and government are the sovereign influence in human society; in the last resort they shape and control it at their pleasure. Institutions depend on them and are by them formed and modified. What they sanction will ever be generally considered innocent; what they condemn is thereby made a crime, and if persisted in becomes rebellion."—Thomas Arnold.

"It is better to allow men to do a great deal of evil than to restrict individual liberty to such a degree that government and law will be looked on as enemies. The evil, if it be plainly such, and yet does not obviously or seriously threaten the existence or the well-being of society, must be endured for the sake of freedom, and be left to society and opinion to correct."—Woolsey, "Political Science," vol. i., p. 232.

"Make it as hard as possible for a man to go wrong, and as easy as possible for a man to go right."—Gladstone.

"But when a sect (reform party) becomes powerful, when its favor is the road to riches and dignities, worldly and ambitious men crowd into it, talk its language, conform strictly to its ritual, mimic its peculiarities, and frequently go beyond its honest members in all the outward indications of zeal. No discernment, no watchfulness on the part of ecclesiastical rulers (party leaders) can prevent the intrusion of such false brethren. The tares and the wheat must grow together. Soon the world begins to find out that the godly are not better than other men, and argues, with some justice, that if not better they must be much worse. In no long time all those signs which were formerly regarded as characteristic of a saint are regarded as characteristic of a knave."—Macaulay.

"The state, in the enactment of its laws, must exercise its judgment concerning what acts tend to corrupt the public morals, impoverish the community, disturb the public repose, injure the other public interests, or even impair the comfort of individual members over which its protecting watch and care are required. And the power to judge of this question is necessarily reposed alone in the legislature, from whose decision no appeal can be taken, directly or indirectly, to any other department of the government. When, therefore, the legislature, with this exclusive authority, has exercised right of judging concerning this legislative question by the enactment of prohibitions like those discussed in this chapter, all other departments of the government are bound by the decision, which no court has a jurisdiction to review."—Bishop on "Statutory Crimes," sec. 995.

"It does not follow that a compulsory law embodies the will of the people, because every man who is opposed to that law is at least ten times more anxious to gain his end than his adversaries are to gain theirs. He is ready to make far greater sacrifices to attain it. One man rather wishes for what he regards as a slight sanitary safeguard ; the other is determined not to submit to a gross violation of his liberty. How differently the two are actuated! One man is willing to pay a farthing in the pound for a desirable object; the other is ready to risk property, and perhaps life, to defeat that object. In such cases as this it is sheer folly to pretend that counting heads is a fair indication of the forces behind. Majorities, for their own sakes, would do well not to bring minorities to bay."—Donisthorpe, "Individualism," p. 46.

"The best way to repeal a bad law is to enforce it."—U. S. Grant.